being an honorary divine
foreigners but that is what it
and write is therefore only th .... the
first circle where black fires rage inconsumably. Candide's
experience of the world is the nearest we can get to the series
of cerebral shocks which await the savage who is earnestly in
search of culture. 'There is nothing here but illusion, and one
calamity after another.' The experience is not unlike that of one
organism living on and at the expense of another.

The ability to read and write exposes the mind to the
haustoria of everything that is written. The parasite is entirely
dependent for food upon our minds. There are very few animals
living in natural conditions which do not possess at least one
parasite, and sometimes a whole fauna is sheltered in various
parts of our thinking. Apart from such ectoparasites as bugs,
like fleas, mosquitoes, leeches, and vampire bats which lead a
free existence but periodically attack the host to suck blood,
there are endoparasites which actually live permanently in our
minds. The latter are also known collectively as 'culture',
'tradition', 'history' or 'civilization'. There is a definite degree of
tolerance established between host and parasite; each becomes
adapted to the other. It is not to the advantage of a parasite to
cause serious harm to its host, as thus it is likely to suffer itself.
To cause the death of its host is tantamount to its committing
suicide. There have been cultures, however, in Germany,
Uganda, Japan, and South Africa which have pig-headedly
embroiled their host in catastrophic strife. Hermann Hesse
sought to escape the social parasite:

> Would you really want
> to be a gentleman now,
> and a master craftsman
> with a wife and children
> reading the paper by the fireside?
>
> Look, said God, I wanted you
> The way you are and no different
> You were a wanderer in my name
> and wherever you went you brought the settled folk
> a little homesickness for freedom.[4]

And in South Africa, Mtshali saw the grim parasitism everywhere:

> Glorious is this world,
> the world that sustains man
> like a maggot in a carcass.[5]

4. Exact source not known.
5. First stanza of O. M. Mtshali, 'High and Low', in: *Poems of Black Africa*, ed. W. Soyinka,
Secker & Warburg, London, 1975, p.293.

Language is like water. You can drink it. You can swim in it. You can drown in it. You can wear a snorkel in it. You can flow to the sea in it. You can evaporate and become invisible with it. You can remain standing in a bucket for hours. The Japanese invented a way of torturing people with drops of water. The Portuguese in Angola and Mozambique also used water to torture people. The dead friend Owen, who painted the mural on my wall, used to dream about putting LSD into South Africa's drinking water. It seems inconceivable to think of humans who have no language. They may have invented gelignite but they cannot do without water. Some take it neat from rivers and wells. Some have it chemically treated and reservoired. Others drink nothing but beer and Bloody Marys and wine but this too is a way of taking your water. The way you take your water is supposed to say a lot about you. It is supposed to reflect your history, your culture, your breeding, etc. It is supposed to show the extent to which you and your nation have developed or degenerated. The word 'primitive' is applied to all those who take their alphabet neat from rivers, sewers, and natural scenery—sometimes this may be described as the romantic imagination. The height of sophistication is actually to channel your water through a system of pipes right into your very own lavatory where you shake the hand of a machine and your shit and filthy manners disappear in a roaring of water. Being water you can spread diseases like bilharzia and thought. Thought is more fatal than bilharzia. And if you want to write a book you cannot think unless your thoughts are contagious. 'Do you still think and dream in your first language?' someone asked me in London. Words are worlds massively shrunk.

> In yonder raindrop should its heart disclose,
> Behold therein a hundred seas displayed.[6]

When thought becomes wisdom, the scholar can say,

> I came like water, and like wind I go.[7]

And the believer can only sing,

> Celestial sweetness unalloy'd
> Who eat thee hunger still;
> Who drink of thee still feel a void
> Which only thou canst fill.[8]

The languages of Europe (except Basque, Hungarian, Finnish, Turkish) are descended from one parent language which was

6. Source not known.
7. E. Fitzgerald, ibid.
8. Source not known.

spoken about 2500 to 2000 BC. This Indo-European group of languages—in their modern form has been carried (by colonization, trade, conquest) to the far corners of the earth. Thus the Indo-European river has quite neatly overflowed its banks and like the flood in the Bible has flooded Africa, Asia, America and all the islands. In this case there does not seem to have been any Noah about who built an ark to save even just two words of all the languages and speech, which were drowned. Literacy today is just the beginning of the story. Words are the waters which power the hydro-electricity of nations. Words are the chemicals that H_2O human intercourse. Words are the rain of votes which made the harvest possible. Words are the thunderstorm when a nation is divided. Words are the water in a shattering glass when friends break into argument. Words are the acronym of a nuclear test site. Every single minute the world is deluged by boulders of words crushing down upon us over the cliff of the TV, the telephone, the telex, the post, the satellite, the radio, the advertisement, the billposter, the traffic sign, graffiti, etc. Everywhere you go, some shit word will collide with you on the wrong side of the road. You can't even hide in yourself because your thoughts think of themselves in the words you have been taught to read and write. Even if you flee home and country, sanity and feeling, the priest and mourners, if any, will be muttering words over your coffin; the people you leave behind will be imagining you in their minds with words and signs. And there will be no silence in the cemetery because always there are burials and more burials of people asphyxiated by words. No wonder it is said,

> In the beginning was the Word,
> And the Word was with God.
> And the Word was God,
> All things were made by him;
> And without him was not any thing made
> That was made.[9]

No wonder too it was said,

> Ah, make the most of what we yet may spend,
> Before we too into the dust descend;
> Dust into dust, and under dust, to lie
> Sans wine, sans song, sans singer, and—
> sans end![10]

9. St John, 1, 1 and 3.
10. E. Fitzgerald, ibid.

Suddenly the other side of the world is only an alphabet away. Existence itself becomes a description, our lives a mere pattern in the massive universal web of words. Fictions become more documentary than actual documentaries. The only certain thing about these world descriptions is the damage they do, the devastation they bring to the minds of men and children. You do not become a man by studying the species but his language. The winds of change have cooled our porridge and now we can take up our spoons and eat it. Go, good countrymen, have yourselves a ball.

My studies have made me my own jester. I cannot say a thing without striking an attitude. I tried to love and found it an attitude deep within myself. I tried to hate and that too I found to be an attitude, nailed firmly down to my gut. Everything is an attitude, a sign. Utterly without depth. Even what we mean is an attitude. Pity, cruelty, good, evil, they are all attitudes, mere jacks-in-the-box that suddenly spring out of me. I woke up one day and looked at the things I had always looked at, things like the sun, the clouds, a street, a dustman, a tree, a toilet roll, a bishop, an overcoat. Each single thing was suddenly an attitude utterly complete in itself, abstracted in its own language. Events also are attitudes made necessary because of all the mass of attitudes that happened before and that happen simultaneously with them. The problem is it's only a soft shell of flesh that encloses hollow worlds without bone. In the morning the dustmen will cart away the remnant. The mortuaries and prisons will be full of all the meat. In the newspapers it's blood, shit and tears. In the music it's a demon. In the schools it's a robot. In the books it's looks are vicious. In the films it's a born loser. Very big with tiny meanings. Hounded thoughts began in Freud's home. One good scratch and the sky bleeds visions. What I am right now is an attitude. The earth is not round, said the madman, because if it was I could then go around it back to where I started when I was stoutly refusing to be conceived in my mother's amorous attitude towards father. It is one flat labyrinth whose single law is that there is no retracing of footsteps. Even if your attitudes and genes have really got you into a mess and you know you are irrevocably lost—what they call 'grown-up'—at least you know you can only go forward through the maze until somebody like Knut Hamsun finds your bleached skeleton and he thinks you are striking an attitude for a medical class and for archaeologists and anthropologists: *Homo Rhodesiensis.* It's the same with countries apart from their queer names. What we were and what we will be is what we are, a mortal attitude. In a way, an eternal attitude. Thoughts that think in straight lines cannot see round corners; the missionaries and teachers saw to that. We were taught to want to go to where a straight line goes and to look back over the shoulder to where straight lines come from.

Logic is an attitude. It freezes us forever in the icy tumult of all the cursed attitudes they stuffed into us. But even where thoughts have died, something ghostly lingers behind. An illumination, a show pregnant with astonishment. As it were a notion of transcendence. Otherwise there would be such a stink of dead and rotting thoughts that the living could not think new thoughts. Think of all the thoughts that are dead since the time man grew tired of his gills and fins and stood up on his hind legs to make the handaxe that would prove to all the other evolving forms of life that he alone was *sapiens*. Straightforward things leave no room for the imagination; they allow no other perspectives. The tyranny of straightforward things is more oppressive and more degrading than such idle monstrosities as life and death, apartheid and beerdrinking, a stamp album and Jew-baiting. One plus one equals two is so irrefutably straightforward that the unborn child can see that even if man was wiped off the face of the earth one plus one would always and forever equal two.

It's a pity nation-making moves only through a single groove like a one-track brain that is obsessed with the one thing. It is not enough to be in power but to be power itself and there is no such thing except in the minds of people with religious notions. We are a devastated garden in a time of drought in which only those weeds grow which are lean and hungry, like Cassius. The multitudes are thick with grey hairs. Their empty bellies propel them to the immediate source. A time will come when their thoughts are not their needs and then I say beware the blazing of their minds.

> Go, borne over the cities of mankind
> On whirlwind-footed coursers: once again
> Outspeed the sun around the orbed world;
> And as thy chariot cleaves the kindling air
> Thou breathe into the many-folded shell,
> Loosening its mighty music; it shall be
> As thunder mingled with clear echoes: then
> Return; and thou shalt dwell beside our cave.[11]

11. P. B. Shelley, *Prometheus Unbound* (1820), Act 3, Scene 2, lines 76–83.

37

It is the force with which the earth attracts. And when soldiers crook fingers about the trigger then it's time for me to give a hearing to another nervous breakdown.

That joke can cure a cobra's bite. Whatever we achieve is the evidence of our guilt. Always we are the desert island for which we secretly pine. There is nowhere to hide on the road to suicide. I have a power for explosive prevarication, like a chair on which all opinions can for a fashion sit. When I was a child I played childishly; when I became a man I put away the ghost of literary thought that stuffed me with attitudes in my student days. What is it, this vast room we call the sky; these endless miles of reality thickly knit with grit? The waiter must stretch his lips if he wants to get the tips. We stand each to each like sides of rock once quarried mercilessly by blind Victorian adventurers who only sought the few gold veins in us. They have extracted the best part of our being and left us like this. I woke up long ago this morning with aches and pains in all the things I took for granted. This desperate tinder becomes youth. Even the death certificate is not quite like me, said Lazarus when he came out of the tomb. Things always happen in the worst possible way, however hard one tries to unbend them. I can never look a rational thought straight in the eyes. Hate me if you wish, but not too offensively. And there I was yesterday hammering the typewriter keys with a worldliness not of this world. Thoughts like claws must be sheathed. Something always happens to show us how really blind we are. This is not only stranger than we imagine but stranger than we can imagine. We cannot all afford the luxury of self-disgust but someone has to do the dirty work. That means—me. My hunger has stamina enough. My actions are always my fault though my thought would plead otherwise. Attitudes—attitudes.

Marota: He has made jokes of us.
Bishop: I'll laugh while it lasts.
Marota: He has sweetened our tea with petty cabinet posts.
Bishop: Then enjoy the invitation and drink the tea.
Marota: But how?
Bishop: Stop fretting.
Marota: He's got us dangling on his hook; For us it's either the frying pan or back to the sea of vagrants and of desperate unemployed.
Bishop: Perhaps it's not a fish he's caught, but something crab-like that will give him nightmares.
Marota: What about the attack on Zambia? He said we all agreed on

Bishop:	it. That cuts us off from whatever support Africa ever gave us. I do not need that kind of support.
Marota:	But the masses—
Bishop:	I am the masses. Did I not rout Pearce? And with placards too. Have I not engineered the first black and white government without a Congo or an Angola? What are you worrying about? I am black and you are black but do I know whether your soul is with the devil or with God? These who strike at the heart of God's country have renounced religion. They are communists. Devils. That is why I agreed to let our troops attack the Zambian bases. *(Music)*
Marota:	You carry your God too high above the trees. The people cannot see him. All they see is the smoke and shrapnel of their own kind being killed at your orders.
Bishop:	I am the people. And I have the best of advisers; that professor who wrote *On Trial For My Country*. Right now I can see myself this day centuries to come being dragged into the dock on trial for God's own country. I see myself being acquitted without stain on my character, which is more than I can say about Lobengula. Africa is faith. Africa is spirit. Africa in its long sweltering breath has always cried out for the heartbroken. For the mind-breaking vision that will soothe the living and the dead. The people are not Godless. This is the mistake you hot-heads always make. (Ah, had we but time enough . . .)
Marota:	Time is what we have not got. The guerillas are pounding on the front door, at the back door, on the roof, and at all the windows. The people still live under the old oppressive laws. They are smouldering in the prisons and in the detention camps. They eke a pitiful living out of the stone of the protected village. The schoolchildren are deserting their schools to join the Patriotic Front. And at the university there is a new and hard edge, cutting the quiet of the campus. We who are now ruling the country alongside the very man who once reviled and spat upon us are not the end but the beginning of a surge towards what I have so far believed unimaginable.
Bishop:	Changes there must be. Yes. But not violent changes. It's at the moment when we are at the threshold of lifting man from the evil of his condition that we suddenly realize the enormous responsibility we have taken upon ourselves. There is no greater chain than freedom. It is a terrible thing. Suddenly, a terrible beauty is born.[12] It is a mark that sets you apart even as Cain was set apart. *(Flourish and shout)* See how they dance and drink their brief minutes. Perhaps not without a care for the morrow. For the most part they are honest, hard-working men. And women. Houseboys, garden boys, factory hands, farmhands, students, teachers, nurses,

12. W. B. Yeats, 'Easter 1916'.

	miners. There are also thieves, pimps, pick-pockets, writers, tsotsis, murderers, liars. But see how eager they are to catch the hour of this day. See how even Smith seems to please them now. It's a sight bold enough to be a foundation for the future. Helen!
Helen:	Yes?
Bishop:	You must not strain yourself. Excitement may hurt the unborn. But mingle more with the women. Speak to them. Sound them out.
Helen:	I will, my lord.
Bishop:	Our women have had the hardest time of it. I shall see that their reward is as great.
Marota:	The pill certainly has not had any effect.
Bishop:	The pill is a European mischievousness. Nature is woman and can look after her own rituals.
Marota:	But girls physically grow more quickly now—
Bishop:	Who knows what women are? Certainly men do not. And I think the women do not know either. After all, birth is a miracle, a sacrament we do not fully comprehend. It is the same with the birth and governance of nation states. I as midwife to my people will do all I can. Is it not said that for evil to prevail it is enough that good men do nothing? Yes, Marota, let us do what we can. Whatever we achieve will be the evidence of our good intentions. (*Enter Smith and his Train*)
Smith:	Pat, do not all these black faces look blank to you? For twelve years I have shouted 'Not In My Lifetime' and tortured them and strung them up on the gallows and starved them and kicked them too when they were down. (*Shouting and music*) I do not understand them. Either they do not have normal feelings of civilized and responsible vengeance or their insides are iron and flint which give out sparks only when you diplomatically clang them together. Like today. How horrible their dancing is!
Pat:	Do not fear them. They are not dangerous.
Smith:	Look at Marota. If I could I would avoid that man. He reads too much. He is a great observer, and he looks quite through the deeds of men. And he is one-half a minister of justice! He loves no plays as you do, Reverend Bishop. He hears no music; seldom smiles, and smiles in such a sort as if he mocked himself and scorned his spirit that could be moved to smile at anything. Come on my right hand, bishop, for this ear is deaf, and tell me truly what you think of him for I don't want him in my cabinet—I mean, our cabinet. (*Exeunt Smith and Bishop and the Train*)
Marota:	Nyanza! Hullo, professor. You look like one who has got VD.
Nyanza:	You look as healthy yourself, Marota. It is a day when sickness shines with health.
Marota:	Anaximander could trace it back to the original sea sickness.
Nyanza:	We shall evolve. We shall evolve.

Marota:	And acquire characteristics too.
Nyanza:	That would be a very long wait.
Marota:	My grey hairs shriek with mineral desire.
Nyanza:	You are the last lingering tooth in the old country's jaw.
Marota:	The worms feed where my sperm decreed.
Nyanza:	The gospel says 'Tommorow homeless who today are reckless';
Marota:	Standing room only at the whiteman's door.
Nyanza:	The Africa that's on the ground floor is a U.F.O.
Marota:	It's the crush in the elevator.
Nyanza:	Is this all that remains of 1896?
Marota:	The part that will leap forward.
Nyanza:	Without looking; what a leap. Here we are in the cactus skin of expediency.
Marota:	Opportunity, too. Let those who will, cool their heels in London.
Nyanza:	They are still my friends.
Marota:	Friends with incredible ends made awkward bed-fellows.
Nyanza:	Our white acquaintances are no less unbelievable.
Marota:	They accommodate us.
Nyanza:	Bed and breakfast with no underdogs or cats allowed. (*Pause*) The missionaries taught me well how to circumvent guilt.
Marota:	Now you teach our children the same lesson.
Nyanza:	Willingly.
Marota:	But they got our bishop hook line and sinker.
Nyanza:	He needs weaning.
Marota:	(*Slyly*) Quite drastically too.
Nyanza:	I will miss him.
Marota:	He is not dead and buried yet.
Nyanza:	He is.
Marota:	Then I spoke to his ghost just now.
Nyanza:	He is doomed to wander forever around our cities giving benedictions to invisible citizens.—Here comes commander Walls. (*Enter Walls*)
Walls:	Nyanza, you look just like an escaped convict who has stolen an academic gown.
Nyanza:	Walls, you are a white wine that has been left open for ninety years.
Marota:	And how are your present duties, Walls?
Walls:	Tedious. I look to the future.
Marota:	The future is our pressing need.
Walls:	My bladder will soon burst if it is not relieved.
Marota:	Are our visitors in the army satisfactory?
Walls:	The mercenaries? They're bloody good. The terrs won't worry us for long.
Marota:	Is their loyalty to you unalloyed?
Walls:	Of course. You just worry about your end of the stick.
Marota:	And Smith? He has not the slightest suspicion about you?
Walls:	No. White faces please him no end. He cannot have enough

of them. He sees himself surrounded by a wall of blank black faces all staring at him. It is you, Marota, whom he fears. Pinkerton, my number two, did have some odd notion or two but I managed to satisfy him. I don't trust him though. True blue and all that. Always quoting Kipling. And very cold about the way things are going. I can handle him though and if necessary arrange a timely accident.

Marota: Anything else I can do for you, Walls?

Walls: No. Our last conversation took care of everything.

Marota: Then come straight tonight to our meeting place. You too, Nyanza. (*Exit*)

Walls: A man of business.

Nyanza: And yet somehow too sharply outlined. He was the same at school: very scant in sport but abundant in conspiracy.

Walls: In Ireland where I come from—(*Sound of footsteps*) Goodnight. (*Exit*) (*Enter Citizen*)

Citizen: You are one of the arse-licking lackeys.

Nyanza: Yes.

Citizen: (*Spits into his face*) That's what I think of it.

Nyanza: But what are you doing about it? Slogans and sauciness are not the stuff of revolutions.

Citizen: Neither is polishing Smith's boots.

Nyanza: (*Smiling*) Perhaps. That puts us on the same level, my friend.

Citizen: So. What then?

Nyanza: (*Aiming a revolver at him*) This! (*Silence*)

Citizen: (*Suddenly*) Shoot me! Shoot me!

Nyanza: I will. (*Shoots*)

Citizen: (*Dying*)

Nyanza: (*Contemptuous*) Get up, you fool. That was a blank. You see you are all talk and attitudes, utterly spineless. You cannot even die like a man. I wanted you to face up to it. To experience the sudden incision of the future. (*He offers the gun to Citizen*) Take it. If you really care about what is happening in our country then take it and use it well. Here are more clips. I will see you later in my office in the Faculty of Arts.

Citizen: (*Taking the gun*) What are you?

Nyanza: A lackey. Now, go back to campus and think out clearly what you will do. It is the quickest way to learn about the institution called Man.

Citizen: How did you know I'm doing anthropology?

Nyanza: I have followed your progress these two years. I like what I see. (*Pause*) Take care. (*Exit Citizen*)

Nyanza: (*Bitterly*) I could not resist such an opportunity. I have learnt nothing and forgotten nothing. Is that what being an educated African means? (*Pause*) After this, let Smith seat him sure, for we will shake him or worse days endure. (*Enter Benzi*)

Benzi: Ah! the very man I was looking for. Has Smith retired? You look like an anaconda that has eaten powdered glass. It's strange, isn't it, that today all our ambitions have borne fruit

	and we are in the government and can sit back to scratch our fleas without a care in the sun. I say, are you all right?
Nyanza:	How are you, Chief Benzi? No, it's not strange at all. Perhaps you have suddenly been given back your eyesight and can see black and white trees walking like men.
Benzi:	You always have your little joke. The other side of the world is suddenly only a mirror away.
Nyanza:	It is the mad gurgle of an abortion being sucked down the plughole of independence.
Benzi:	Look at them. The path to the front door tells a wretched martyred lot where no half-naked multitude peering from mud-huts dispute in negro spirituals the bustle of life beyond.
Nyanza:	This, Chief, is the ease with which patience drains out of the gashes in our wrists. It frames beyond recognition our embittered days together.
Benzi:	The only solution is: don't be black where brains and scanty hair come away with the Afro comb. (*Pause*) On which garden shall we pour the bucket of power? On the blackjacks that for so long have strived alone to grow and stick out their furry seeds like so many thumbs wagging on the road for a single lift? Or shall we tilt the bucket on the Marimba daisies which have always had the coin but not the right shade of skin? And when the bucket is empty and the gardener struts back to the source shall he find Smith controlling the tap, or perhaps the bishop, or perhaps the minions of the Patriotic Front? Have you no ends in view? There is something unyielding in you which only a man of action has. I do not doubt the spring of your spear if ever the need arises.
Nyanza:	I merely scratch my fleas without a care, Chief. But you seem to be bowed down with cares all of a sudden. Enjoy yourself while it lasts. It's not that often that blacks and whites rub backsides in the same seats of government. Soon we shall have our one-man one-vote—if we behave ourselves. Drink and dance, Chief, hug and fuck, sign and cheer, for, as you said, our ambitions have this day borne fruit.
Benzi:	But the bishop—
Nyanza:	Sod the bishop, my good chief. The church always dirties its finger in the right pie. We're all equal now, Chief. You can go and drink Castle in Meikles. Do you know what Smith thinks? He thinks you and I are ignorant, greedy, lecherous, stinking, back-stabbing, tribalistic wogs. We'll show him he's wrong, won't we? We'll be whiter than white from now on. We'll be more civilized than civilization itself. We'll out-progress progress itself. We'll be honest to goodness, spick and span, lobster and caviar knights of this city. Those dogs in London, who are spreading lies and slander about us and the little bishop and writing books about it, have run out of time. They're no longer relevant to the spikenard of this our God's own country. We have come into a time of critical frankness. Tell me: am I wrong or am I right? Come, we'll go to Meikles right now and drink each other's health. (*Exeunt*)

It is Wednesday. There is a bomb on our roof. It dropped there on Sunday night. When I climbed on to the roof to look at it I could hear a faint humming sound purring inside it. The planes came over early in the evening on a bombing run. When they had finished, the fire that had broken out lit up the ruins of the city and it was eerie. I have never lived under the shadow of a bomb before.

When the news of the bomb spread about the house, a hush seethed in all the rooms and corridors. You could hear how there is no silence when sound ceases. I had a mild attack of palpitations and I could not erase out of my mind the bitterness from the bitter pictures of war which I suddenly remembered. Vietnam. Korea. Kolwezi. Soweto. Dresden. Hiroshima. War is no longer a mere fact of life but life itself. It is no longer a shadow under which we live; now it is us. Perhaps it has always been so, the only difference being that we no longer even care to waste our breath justifying our actions. A toothless speech-lessness chewed its gum in the interior of the house. The ear-splitting stillness gnawed shrilly at the lattices of the brain.

The woman and the child introduced themselves as Liz and Henry. The boy was quite excited by the bomb on our roof. I gave him a pile of war comics from the old days. Nazis screaming Achtung! and Japs coming over a hill shouting Banzai! Bayonets like steel erections rape the enemy in one gigantic orgasm, making sure that once more Empire and Common-wealth are safe. One of my uncles actually served in the Sahara and in Burma. He is now shrunken and old, just another old black man squatting in his mud-hut and complaining that the young (meaning me) do not care about the virtues and adventures and pathos of war. What he means, I suppose, is that the self-dramatization necessary in any corporate outrage no longer reeks of significance in our youth's nasal frankness. But war has actually become a fact of life in our own time. The good old missionary-in-a-stewing-pot diplomatic complication being cleared up by paras from Tel Aviv is now a situation overtaken by the new militarized anarchy. However, a tongue-in-cheek attitude is the only sane one when confronting the subject of aggression.

And Liz was quite aggressively human today.

She finished another bout of sweeping the corridors and then tirelessly made a pot of tea and miraculously produced sugar and milk and cakes and we were all invited to her 'apartment'. It was the first time I had really met some of my neighbours, and just the sight of them told me why.

44

Cicero, my neighbour who is always shouting obscenities about the 'warmongering' bastards, actually wears a toga and bowler hat. He walked into the room like a Royal Shakespearian Company public relations stunt. He, in fact, studied at RADA and did some minor roles in *The Satyricon* and in *The Golden Ass* for an obscure provincial company in the backyard of Scotland. He showed me some news cuttings of the event. He is in his late forties, grey and balding, and has the most expensive looking tic on the left half of his clean-shaven face. There is in his right eye a dusky Latin glint which is perpetually piercing the marrow of whomever he is talking to. I liked him, from the start, especially when he buttonholed me into a corner and neatly got me into a good stranglehold of a conversation:

'Real life being the essence of drama,' he said, 'means every instant of our lives is a complete play in itself. Our very bodies are composed of neat cellular dramas whose total tumult is a man in the act of saying 'I am ill' or 'Good evening'. These stones upon which we stand and call planets and mine and grind them into settings for our human dramas are themselves always in the act of their own dramas, spinning round the sun and eclipsing and disintegrating into meteorites. While we, immersed in the minutes of our last rehearsals (what we call tradition, civilization) think only of our own lines and footnotes, perhaps the grand drama of all the things we do not take into account is itself approaching a climax whose debris and shrapnel will devastate us.'

I shook my head up and down, from side to side.

'What are pinpricks in the evolution and decline of the universe are, of course, matters of importance to the human cycle of "miracle" play,' I said, rather astonished at myself. But I went on: 'Human beings have only been here on earth since the Pleistocene era. Soon in a couple more millions of years we will probably die out as the dinosaur epic is said to have done, though fresh evidence has shown that some of that species did evolve into the birds we know today.'

'A great deal of our plays derive their strength from what I call "The Act of Summing Up" whereby the playwright deliberately sums up in enlightened dramatic syntax, the language and signs of his day or age. The past, which is already solidly enlightened by six feet of dust, is therefore the natural subject of an apprentice writer. I have heard your typewriter night after night hammering away at the tombs of the past.

'If you look through a camera lens down at a busy street full of pedestrians and shoppers and trucks and robberies and coronations and dustmen and in a calculated moment press the shutter freezing all that activity on to a photographic plate and you then develop it and look at the picture—what do you call that? Do you say you have the past in your hands? An inkling of the future, perhaps? Or the present? At what instant does time or timelessness divide itself into past, present and future? What of the state of the universe at precisely the moment the shutter fell? The stars that we see, some of them strike our eyes with light for the first time hundreds of years after that light in them was born. For instance, Rigel, which is more than 900 light years away, appears to us exactly as it was in 1066. And in spite of our poetic imaginations about the sun, we only actually see it eight and a half minutes late from a distance of some 93 million miles. Rigel we see 900 years late. And so on, etc, etc. The same complexity is deep-seated in man himself. In his presentation of himself when he is born and when he dies. In his acting out the prismatic effect of himself every instant of his lifetime.

'Yet a man is not even his own spectator, however much he thinks so. Talk of self-realization and "identity" and their attendant pathos and banality are the poorest of summings-up. The lens entightens the activity of the stress and yet also a glance at the photograph shows us how limited that is. The mental heights and cerebral corrosions going on in the brains of the subject are what the spirit or soul is. Emaciation or obesity may physically express it. But deep down in the cornerstones of the tiny organisms and cells that in sum are our corporate state that same state of being is being expressed perhaps in other terms. Terms, other than pain and terror, or the highly-charged carthartic element an imbecile audience demands. Don't you think?' he asked.

'Just as the skin of water supports a multitude of insect and other life, in the same way dramatic syntax carries on its surface complex and minute sensations of space, time, etc. which deep beneath the surface are as awful and mysterious as the deepest fraction at the bottom of the deepest sea,' I replied. 'In a way we are no longer talking about the common plays of theatre and stage but of the very activity of life and non-life itself. Is it not strange and uncommon that we can talk like this in the very midst of bombs and bullets and disease? It is not. The imagination reaches only that which is just beyond the grasp of human capability. No more. If our acts were really strange to ourselves and to our imagination then we would indeed understand what insanity is. For we conduct ourselves in terms of clarity and stability and roses which are only a minute fraction of the spectrum of the impossible and the possible. Hence such of what we know of as real life is limited within the thin thread of colour in which we have positioned ourselves in the spectra of the universe.'

I could hear myself getting carried away by the twitching of the left half of his face and the shimmering dusky glint in his right eye. The Ancient Mariner, of Coleridge's imagination, was not so ancient after all. There he was, mesmerizing me with the articulate eccentricity of my anti-war neighbour. He might have been something like Conrad's *Nigger of the Narcissus* or Melville's multi-tattooed harpooner if that bowler hat and the toga had not recalled to me a picture of Caligula strutting through the decline and fall of Rome, mouthing exterminations in a Viennese accent. The cut of his toga was impeccably regal, the shell-eared serrations of his advancing years gave him the air of one who lives forever. Bernard Shaw's *Back to Methuselah* could explain a third of his overall effect on me. But he was speaking:

'I have seen something of the long hard years and they still flow around me as though I was a fish in their water. I fear death by drowning in one of T. S. Eliot's poems and yet here I am perfectly capable of breathing in the underwater of time. The paradox applies to all who care to apply it. And we do apply it in literature and drama with drenching gasps of intervals, of course. We swim in sanity like crabs perfectly at home in water and yet amphibious when we choose. Here we are drinking tea in a plague-ridden house surrounded by war. Do you know what this building is? It was part of the university. Yes. The Faculty of Arts. When the war came out of the blue sky like something out of Ixtlan, only more deadly than the lessons Castaneda learnt, it destroyed most of the buildings and what was left of the intellectual atmosphere was this plague-ridden building with its diseased ghosts of arts' undergraduates still wandering about in the corridors waiting for tutorials and seminars that were never to come. Waiting until today. In a way, you and I are conducting a sort of tutorial, a better one at that than the usual rigmarole.'

Liz who had come over during his speech and seemed ill or overcome by something which was wet and bloodshot in her gold-earing eyes, suddenly said:

'I used to teach here. Old English and Medieval Literature. My office was right in the room you are staying in, you know.'

'Indeed—my room?' I murmured.

'Yes. I shared it with Brown who did Twentieth Century.'

For the first time I looked at her, seeing her as she was. A thin face and thin stringy hair, both set precariously on an onion-shaped body that rested uneasily on a pair of thin scanty legs. The gold-earing eyes squinted with myopia. But it was her ears which struck me most about her. They were a shrunken version of the elephant kind, waving slightly with the rise and fall of her carefully modulated voice. It was an uneasily plastic voice that sounded to the inner ear like empty plastic bags being squashed suddenly. And she was pale, paler than the whitest ghost in a girls' romance. Her long slender fingers were almost transparent. Looking at her thin wispy hair, and at her thin white face that was set like a skin of water, you could have sworn that you could see the fragile skull underneath and even the grey impression of the brain imprinted eerily on the weak-seeming skull.

I sipped at the tea cup that was empty in my hands.

'I never quite succeeded in communicating to my students the overwhelming power and interest of Anglo-Saxon poetry, but I helped them pass the time I suppose. You are Mr—'

'Cicero,' he said.

She did not even blink.

'I must read your works sometime,' she said.

'I have not finished them yet. They require a great deal of revising and simplifying if anyone other than myself is to understand them.'

'Publishers and editors are a problem, are they not, Mr Cicero?'

'They are not my problem,' he replied smiling.

'And you, Mr—?'

'Marechera,' I said. As she sipped her tea I thought for one ghastly moment that I could actually see (as she swallowed it) the tea going down into her in one evergrowing brown stain so pale and pink was her beaux-arts frock.

'What do you do?'

'Stories, fictions,' I said vaguely.

She looked vaguely at my face over the rim of her extended finger.

'Those who do, do; those who can't, teach,' she said and

48

added wonderingly: 'I've never met any black writers. Are you angry and polemic or are you grim and nocturnal or are you realistic and quavering or are you indifferent and European? Those are the categories, I think,' she said and neat creases delicately bracketed her wide mouth.

'I write as best I can,' I replied, at a loss for words.

'Perhaps Mr Cicero knows,' she suggested.

'I have never read any of his work,' he said.

'There's lots more tea, everyone,' she breathed to the rest of the gathering.

I refilled my cup and as I did so a girl's hand reached out from nowhere and touched my face. It was the fourteen-year-old who was soon to become fifteen. As Liz and Cicero seemed on the brink of a conversational wrestling match which I did not think he would win, I sat on a cushion in front of the girl and stirred a cup, wondering at the confusion inside me.

'What is your name?' I asked.

To know the name of a demon is supposed to give one power over it. But names are so prosaic and final; they leave no room for any other dream. There was a missionary who knew an African called Flying Machine; others like myself chose other facets of English hegemony and were christened Charles, William, Patrick or Dereck, etc. The English language has certainly taken over more than the geography of the African image.

But she was looking at me mischievously with her sad eyes which now looked pale aquamarine rather than the emeralds of my late thinking of her.

'Helen,' she said.

Biting her lip half-bashfully, half-provocatively, she stirred her tea without looking at the cup. I was sure now, but not of her feelings which I knew nothing about and did not want to know. There is something best left unsaid about feelings which has a great deal to do with whatever was happening between us. In fact I cannot express this demanding element of it which was sweet and bitter like the stinging of pain and thyme. Or the inside-out spent yearning which tempers the affections and wrings them with a tenacious tenderness. She was so young— at the same time so old!

'Can I move in with you?' she asked quietly.

The tea on my tongue was suddenly a remote and indifferent taste from another world where Boston Tea Parties helped shape the destiny of nations and India and the East was an unheard-of desert island only found in the annals of traders and Marco Polos. At the same time it struck me how it could possibly not be so. Genghis Khan reading Thomas Love Peacock could not have been more astonished.

'Of course, Helen,' I said as though I had been saying that all my life. 'Straightaway if you like. Or I could put the place into shape for you. And you can move in then.'

'You left the door open when you came here,' she said. 'I've already put my things there. I brought lots of blankets. You don't seem to have enough. And I brought some things for us to eat without actually going hungry like you seem to have been doing. Lots of muesli and cereal from my old place.'

She added hastily:

'I won't disturb your writing at all. I know how not to. And it's important you must go on writing. I will be doing my drawing. I draw quite well but not yet as well as I want to so I have lots there to do. Liz knows what's wrong with me. I am not actually insane or mentally retarded. It's something inherited which is a long word I cannot pronounce but Liz can and she said if I ever cause you any disquiet you are to speak to her, tell her because she knows what to do to bring me round again.'

'Do you hurt? Are you in pain? What is it?'

'It hurts sometimes, like a splitting headache all over inside me. I get dizzy then. Sort of subtracted from the world by the pain. But that isn't as bad as it sounds. I'm used to it.'

Suddenly the tea had really gone cold. I shivered. She was looking at me intently, clearly, sadly. Her voice came from the other edge of the world:

'Hey; are you all right?'

I remembered what I had written about her in the slick and hypocritically honest way about 'invisible wound bleeding in her mind' to make her like that.

'I'm okay,' I said hoarsely.

I must have sounded totally absorbed by her for she shook her head the way you shake off incredulity with a slight delicate toss of her long silver hair.

'Welcome home,' I added inadequately.

And she kissed me right between the eyes where it hurt. The sound of a match being scratched alight was the tearing inside my head. It lit the half-darkness of my knowledge of her. In the same instant she knew that I was sure, now.

'I'll go lie down a bit,' she said. 'And don't talk to her long because I'll be waiting in there alone for you.'

I did mean to talk to Liz about her. I said:

'You go on then. I won't be long.'

I watched her go.

I had never 'understood' women and I am never likely to. I detest understanding anyone that way. I cannot even say I know anything about my feelings for particular women. I usually close the subject to myself by saying that I do not want to know. From late adolescence I had been severally in love with them without ever knowing why or how it could be. It had been ugly and beautiful and demoralizing and exciting all at the same time. Perhaps I was too early in contact with the bookish nature of it all. Even Jane Austen's notions about it among the landed gentry and middle class was as much a textbook of it as *Wuthering Heights* and *Jane Eyre*. At the same time there was the Dickensian lorgnette of it; the Lorna Doones and Becky Sharps; and the *Middlemarch* versions and they were all somehow mixed up with the more masculine preoccupations of heroism, manhood, trial by strength which in effect led to ideas about worthiness and unworthiness. And there was the Henry James effect which at once elevated it and curiously enough debased it. It all led back to dissections of art and artistic feeling especially the type in Thomas Mann where disease and corruption or consumption are at the very guts of beauty.

At the same time I was then growing up in the very midst of the cultural cerebral rape of my people and political awareness in the form of large-scale reading of the subject informed me somewhat about how my own mind was and was being shaped. Since then I have always feared those things which malevolently tamper with the mind and the feelings and, if I was in the Orwellian *1984*, Big Brother would probably subdue me quite easily by threatening to perform some kind of brain operation on me. It is not sanity or insanity that I fear but the power that consciously shapes these in others. Advertisements, educational programmes, television, the radio, universities, general elections, wars and the very notion of progress have performed mass brain operations in the heads of peoples in Africa, America, Asia and the Pacific. The human being consciously created himself by cramming inside his own head the things that have convinced him of his separateness from his animal lineage. In the same way, others today are convincing themselves in Africa and elsewhere of their own elite separateness

51

from those 'unfortunate' enough not to have had brain operations quickly enough, if ever. In this maze I only know that the presumption of superior intelligence is more likely to hurt than to heal, more likely to dehumanize than to make us more human. Indeed, the more ferocious wars among us have come only with the introduction and increase of schools and churches and universities.

Yes, I watched her go with something like self-loathing.

I was wondering how soon I would stop seeing her and only see the idea of her in my own head. It has always struck me that men and women are only ideas in each other's heads. Even when the hatred or the love is so strong it could melt steel, we still continue to hate and to love the idea and not the flesh which seems gross and mortal and beautiful and sometimes like the genitals just crudely there. There is such about the body which even a tried liberal would automatically label obscene or unthinkable in a sexual way. The quibbling about whether it should be in public or in private merely avoids the issue which is that the human body has a lot of orifices and appendages which sexually arouse feelings. The pretence of wearing clothes and therefore denying the body always suffers the fate of the emperor, but most of us only meet that fate when a sister or a daughter is suddenly pregnant and unmarried or when little children experiment behind bushes or when incest or other more callous outrage happens. But the emperor's fate is more often met in the love and domestic dramas of our society and, in fact, the mainstay of the divorce courts and crimes of passion and the attendant industry in psychiatry and psychoanalysis; it is there at the centre of literature which naively continues to wear clothes even though they are more obscene than the physical charms which are supposed to be hidden for the censor's benefit. To mentally strip naked all the people at a tea party and having done so to listen attentively to their conversation and to note their gestures and movements whether standing or sitting is a sobering lesson which ought to be done more often. A naked man cannot have any statues but himself; clothed and belted he wields a power which is sickening to behold.

The psychology of clothes has a great deal to do with why men submit to brain transplants in whatever guise of colonialism they may be operated. The mind is like a man's innermost treasure; he shows it to others if he knows that in their terms it is also a treasure. Approval, acceptance, praise are not always what men seek but a man occasionally needs some of them. Hence—when thoughts are no longer needs then perhaps a terrible beauty would have been born. But this too is to clothe things a little in the Yeats kind of phrase which was not always appropriate. But Yeats dealt with the kind of harbours in which his sensibility could take refuge from the literal strait-jackets of his time and world. His achievement was that—having failed to find any after strenuous and symbolic search, he turned round to face the bear and the storm, and perished?

Oscar Wilde was not at all so fortunate. Refusing to sheathe the claws of his thought and sexuality, he disdained harbours and found himself a spectacle thrown to the lions in the human arena. *Dorian Gray* is a novel I much admire. *The Ballad of Reading Gaol* and the essays *De Profundis* show us what we missed because his contemporaries chose to drive their most intelligent man on to the rocks. The secret of homosexuality in E. M. Forster's life seems also to have stunted and finally silenced his talent, to our great loss. De Sade had to become at home in France's lunatic asylums before he could write the eloquent bile he understood to be in the arteries of the Parisian psyche. A host of men and women of ideas contrary to the game of actually seeing the emperor's clothes have always been and are being persecuted. News has reached us that Kenya is holding in detention its foremost novelist. Nigeria did the same thing once with Soyinka. South Africa has always done so with its black writers and journalists. Everywhere society demands that the illusion of the clothes be closely observed even though everyone, including the emperor or field marshal, knows that this is mere pretence. The art of the invisible demands many tailors: teachers, lecturers, jurists, scientists, stockbrockers, administrators, and government cabinets, they all assist in creating the wonder-garment of institutions, traditions, precedents, laws, which the long line of citizens will cheer as soon as the emperor or president emerges out in the open to show his new clothes.

I watched her go without misgiving.

When I turned I almost collided into a dog-eared man who stood apart from the rest. He was dressed in black Elizabethan dress, like a single-handed performance of Hamlet on a cramped stage. I had seen him some mornings and nights sallying forth into the war-torn outside as though something out there irresistibly called to him. He was of middle height, coal black, disillusioned, transfigured, damned, and as it seemed prey to his nerves. I was to learn that he was a barrister who had somehow seen an inexplicable light on his way to the courts and had from that time totally changed his life. He did not so much believe in anything as in the uselessness of human beings in so far as their condition was a kind of predestined horror. For instance, the bomb on our roof did not surprise or affect him in any sense. In my case it had Helen decide to 'move in with me'. It had also made most of us social in the emperor's clothes sense, though that was Liz's doing.

This black Hamlet said his name was Otolith meaning a kind of minute calcareous body that makes it possible for a fish to be conscious of its position in space. Under the influence of gravity otoliths will press downward. As the position of the body moves, they will come in contact with certain sensory hairs in the ampullae, thus causing impulse to be transmitted to the brain by the auditory nerve. Because of the arrangement of the three canals in the three planes of space—from the dorsal part of the vestibule to the utriculus—provision is made for sensation of movements in all directions. When the dogfish starts or ceases to move, a flow is set up in the endolymph, and causes stimulation of the sensory epithelia lining the canals. In this way the otoliths enable the miniature shark to appreciate its position, even when stationary, while the flow of endolymph in canals gives a sense of balance during movement. And I almost collided into him.

'Sorry,' I said.

I was about to pass but something in his manner stopped me. It was as though he had not seen me or heard me or even felt my presence. Even if he was blind—he was not—I had brushed by him and surely he would have felt that. In a sense this was vanity on my part. To be so totally out of somebody else's picture blew me to smithereens. Besides, he gave the impression of being a kind of German Zeppelin balloon just hovering there like a predestined time-bomb among human affairs. And Zeppelins were rather inviting targets for the biplane in the clouds—if the red baron was preoccupied elsewhere. (The little boy, Henry, was still devouring the pile of war comics I had given him.) Anyway, Helen had left me somewhat off balance and that usually makes me reckless. He was turned slightly away from me, his ear invitingly there. I shouted:

'Ahoy, there, Silver!'

I had almost expected the parrot to cry:

'Ten pieces of eight! Ten pieces of eight! Ten pieces of eight!'

The startled silence was like a blow in my guts. I must have been nuts, mixing the Hollywood Lone Ranger with Captain Silver of *Treasure Island*; but both belonged to a time in my growth when I had firmly believed that Bristol was the kind of city I would like to have been kidnapped to. I did not know much about the slave trade then. Right now I did not know where to hide my head except in sudden explanation.

'That bomb is driving me nuts,' I said.

'Anyway,' I added, 'I was thinking of the six who passed while the lentils boiled. When the queen feared she would have her head cut off.'

He frowned, trying to remember.

'We did that at school once,' he said, 'Let me see. Ah, Stuart Walker of portmanteau plays. I would have given anything to be the butterfly but that, of course, is impossible. Who were you?'

'The dreadful headsman.'

'A most realistic character. I once had the honour of meeting one of Zambia's executioners. A white chap. He had just retired and returned to pastures green in Rhodesia on a fat pension. He gave a most entertaining grisly picture of the gallows. He had with the patronage of the government there executed some three hundred black condemned men. They were all kinds— murderers, armed robbers, rebels, rapists. Now he is himself tormented by gout and ulcers and worries more about his wine and food than all the ghosts of the men he hanged. What kind of a man becomes an executioner, do you think?'

I frowned, trying to think.

'Unimaginative,' I replied. 'Without funds. Practical. Totally unsentimental. One who is not his father or his mother unless they too had been in the trade.'

But he shook his head.

'It takes an awful lot of humanity to execute another human being. This particular white hangman in the employment of a black government was extremely imaginative, of independent means (at the beginning), crassly romantic, and doted on his mother. In spite of all this he was good at his job and never pretended to hate it. After all, it was well paid. Everything, almost, has its price. Besides, what the law chooses to do—in

55

the name of justice backs the likes of him up to the hilt. And the law is, of course, the opinion of the citizen. And the citizen in Africa will not, of course, be denied his right to witness public executions, public scourgings, public amputations, public castrations, as long as some court or other has sentenced the victim to that. I was a barrister. I still am but I no longer practise. I found out too late that I was of a timid and squeamish nature. I could not face the fact that the law is merely a screen behind which many a villain lurks. More crimes are committed within the law than against it. It is big business in Kenya. It is big business in Nigeria. In fact there is not one place in our continent where it is not so. Now and then the voice of which Gabriel Okara spoke speaks out but always, as with Kafka, in vain.'

He nibbled at a biscuit like a fish gnawing at the bait. I was scrutinizing the little exclamation marks of weariness which gleamed deep in the wrinkles of his face. In that Elizabethan costume he could fancifully have been the horror which Kurtz saw at the *Heart of Darkness* Brussel's suburbia, encountering the real noble savage, in the person of a burnt-out case clutching Africanity in one hand and a bottle of whisky in the other, had its worst fears realized. And with what irony too! It somehow recalled to me a chance meeting in London with a very old friend whom I had not seen for five years. I had last seen him in the thick of tear gas canisters exploding and police dogs biting at our buttocks and hands. I had left the country. And suddenly one surprisingly hot spring afternoon five years later outside Dillons, where I had just sold a couple of review books to make ends meet, there he was indolently glancing at the pavement and smoking a Benson & Hedges. In the middle of all those crowds he and I somehow were 'cool' towards each other. We had been best friends—were we still that? I was suddenly conscious of my missing front teeth.

'Hello,' I said.

'Hi, man.'

'It's good to see you. I heard you'd come over but no one knew where you are staying.'

'I came up to Oxford last year. Heard about you. Sorry and all that. But congrats about the book. Suppose it's coming out soon?'

'Yes. Do you have any cigarettes?'

He proffered the packet.

At the same instant we both broke out laughing. I was the one who was always broke, always pig-headedly in trouble, and a cigarette from a friend was a ritual which had become so rare in my life that it serves as a psychologically reassuring ceremony. At the same time I could see that he felt slightly uneasy about how I felt about him. I had been a kind of hothead (as the bishop would say) whereas his father was a policeman and he always felt that somehow he must show that he was as truly radical as all the other radicals. I had been out of smokes such a long time that I swayed slightly from the dizziness. The concern showed in his face; I was even more hungry than I had thought.

'What the hell! Come on, let's go to a pub for some grub and a pint. Not the Marlborough, no. Do you know a good one?'

'Down there in Bloomsbury Way.'

'It's fucking good to see you, man. I'm tired of the hypocrites.'

'Then I may be bad company,' I said. 'Writing has made me the worst kind of hypocrite—an honest one.'

He grinned:

'We shall see.'

It was some two hundred yards to get to Bloomsbury Way. Gower Street had its usual sprinkling of little groups huddled around bus stops. This time I had only been in London some four weeks. I had hitch-hiked down from Wales where I had spent three months in prison for possessing cannabis but when I came out I had stayed with an Italian friend who was still trying to make up his mind to write the definitive novel in the Günter Grass manner. Actually I only met Pasquale after I had been evicted from my Cardiff room by my West Indian landlord and had gone to a pub to drink the problem away. My luggage I had thrown into the nearest dustbin, muttering something shit about the West Indies and all I had to carry was my typewriter and books. I had received three rejection slips from poetry magazines and was beyond caring about what would happen to me. There was a group playing darts. I soon joined them as I had a notion that a black man playing darts is received less resentfully by the white working class. Pasquale (the Italian) and I were soon deep in conversation of the literary crit type and we retired to stand at the bar talking.

His immense affection for Günter Grass and Mervyn Peake was infectious. But I had to find somewhere to stay for the night. I asked him.

'What happened at your place?' he asked.

'West Indian landlord,' I said shortly.

'They are the worst ones,' he agreed.

'Threw me out. I threw my luggage away, except for that rucksack which has my books and typewriter. I'm just getting bloody drunk. I don't want to think. Thinking is what gets me into a spot all the time. If you think, they think you are deep. If you don't think, they think you are always half asleep. I was never trained for anything but reading books I like. I haven't the nerve to present myself at a building site as that grossly underrated man, the unskilled labourer. Tried it once and got beaten up. The only thing I can do, I suppose, is to teach but I detest teaching. I'd hate to have the next generation's nightmares on my conscience. Not that I have a conscience. I can't afford one. I have a sort of bellows which puffs up the forge of my mind now and then about issues like obscenity or squatting or the next meal's imponderable absence. I came up from London where a meagre advance from my publisher saved me from the terror of Trafalgar Square when I was sleeping out in St James's Park and evading homosexual advances from the kind of guys who feed on homeless hippie types! I had gone there to sign the contract about the book and get the advance but time didn't seem to move and I didn't want to go to any of the other blacks I knew were in London. It's one thing to be comrades against whites and it's totally another thing to be penniless; the comrades would be suddenly struck by amnesia as far as knowing you went. So I hung around Trafalgar Square and St James's Park and there were hundreds like me without a penny or a roof anywhere in the world. I don't know how many times I stared at the pictures in the National Art Gallery. Or at the pigeons shitting on Nelson's head. And at the lions against which so many tourists were always being photographed. Until then I had forgotten what it means to be hungry and tired of the world. I was sorely tempted to sell my typewriter and my books.

'Then a black policeman stopped me one morning in St James's Park. He demanded to search the rucksack. I first told him what was in it. Then he searched, throwing my things on to the ground and the increasing flow of tourists and sightseers gave us a wide berth. I wondered exactly what it was that all those white faces were seeing as they stared at the black policeman and the black hitch-hiker. It wasn't very flattering. My dirty socks and underpants. My books and manuscripts. The typewriter and my thick-lensed spectacles. Next, he searched me, feeling up from my ankles up to my crotch and then around my hips up to the armpits. He was not satisfied. There was the question of identification. I told him I had come to London from Oxford to sign the contract for my book which was to be published. He looked at the dirty grey hair on my dirty black head. His own was smart—legally groomed. He looked at my jeans and waistcoat and T-shirt; they were filthy beyond belief from sleeping on the ground in the rain with only the branches of trees to keep out the wetness. He demanded to see my letters from Heinemann. I gave them to him. He smiled a sort of Kojak wry smile and said sternly "Keep out of trouble" I stuffed my things back into my rucksack. I had just about had enough. I knew I was going to start shouting insults and raving. But some instinct for survival made me keep my mouth shut and not even watch the black policeman's departure. I suppose my uncombed hair had probably suggested to him that I was a rastafarian but I didn't care. It was only sixteen more hours before the next morning when I would present myself in Charles Street to sign that blasted contract and get the advance and dust my feet of London. I wanted to get to Wales here where a woman I knew was teaching in the university. In Aberystwyth. That night there was a concert in a nearby hall. All the down and out youths with their rucksacks were sitting on the steps. I joined them. Stale bread was passed around. From mouth to mouth. We were there until the sun rose.'

Pasquale finished his pint. I bought the next round. I had not talked to anyone like this for a long time. Things had not worked out with Patricia in Aberystwyth. I had been shocked at how changed she was. She on her part had been shocked at the change in me. I suppose it's one thing to get to know each other in the nowhere of Central Africa and its another thing to think that things will be the same in the United Kingdom. I do not think we had both changed at all; we were only seeing each other incisively for the first time. In any case, the visit was doomed from the start. There was another man with her. She asked him to go into the kitchen while she and I straightened things out.

'You ought to have written to let me know you were coming,' she said.

'There wasn't time. Things were somewhat rough in London

and I felt I had to see you. You were the only connection I had with the past and with what is happening now.'

'It's not been easy, you know,' she said. 'You can't just bosh things up like you did at Oxford and expect me to pick up the pieces. I need picking up myself. And he did. The man in the kitchen. I don't love him and I don't love you. And I don't even love myself. There are too many things to do without that coming in. I did that last summer.'

She was pointing at the oil painting hanging on the wall.

'Do you like?'

I looked at it and admitted that it was good.

'Look,' I said, 'I am here anyway. So let's make the best of it. I've hitched all the way from London and I need a wash and change. I got that advance today. It will keep me some time. Let's go out later and celebrate.'

'All right. Roget!'

The man stuck his head out of the kitchen doorway.

'Go away now,' she said, 'I'll be busy for the next—how long do you intend to stay anyway?'

'For as long as I can stick it,' I said.

'You hear that, Roget? Go away, now.'

The man closed the front door softly.

'Come here,' she said and when I did she shook her head sadly: 'You're a wreck. And to think you once fought to the death a pack of right-wing dogs over my body! You should look after yourself better than that. But don't worry. We will celebrate. And there's lots of hash in there. Roll yourself one if you like. What's that stink? My cakes are burning!'

And she rushed into the kitchen.

I slowly rolled myself a joint.

'How did you cope when I left?' she shouted from the kitchen.

'I finished the book and sent it to the publishers.'

'I knew you'd make it. You've got so many words inside your head like a sort of writing sausage machine. Do you like burnt cakes? Try them anyway. After all if you'd married me you'd have to eat them.'

I went into the kitchen. They were marijuana cakes. They weren't burnt at all. The kitchen was glinting with hundreds of little jars filled with herbs. It was like being in a unique witch's library. Already I could feel the disappointment melting away way down in that little gut where I am not as pessimistic as I would like to be. Even her club foot seemed changed. The wind driving in from the sea brought into the room a faint fragrance of things long dead and gone. I parted the curtains and looked out. It was raining a little. The wind had whipped up the waves into a tumultuous frenzy of leap and spray. Though it was warm in the room, I felt a sudden chill trickling through the marrow of my bones. There was nothing out there or inside me which I could see was the wire between the life inside me and the actual geography of living. Even then, by life I meant the discontent and the erased feelings which presented themselves only in logical situations. There was something more which did not (perhaps could not) come to the fore of my consciousness but only stirred and bristled when in the presence of deep and faraway things, like the sea or Snowdon or the rugged and rocky shore where the waves could only forever hurl themselves achingly to dash their brains out of the water. So many words inside their whip and leap. So many feelings subtracted out of my world. This was the tearing cloth of exile, and of the sense of being in a world in which one yearned to leap out of one's mind. But the inexorable equation had long been set and by it one could discover that feeling of inhuman balance and inhuman space which holds our humanity. The syntax of the nausea is the ballast of the submarine. To throw the levers wide open and let the damnation sink with one to the grim bottom of the sea would leave pearls where our eyes once were. So much emotion subtracted from the wind.

'You could join us at the community centre,' Pasquale said. 'We're short of teachers there.'

I taught twice a week there. It was not much fun. My students were mostly adult Asian men and women and I was there to teach them to speak read and write English. In the meantime I stayed at Pasquale's flat where we spent the nights and days talking about music and art and books. I began writing for the local newspaper but it was not easy because so much of it had to be tamed and toned down and I did not like that.

We turned into Bloomsbury Way. Minutes later we had settled in a window-seat and were sipping Burton Ale while munching sandwiches. He rolled his eyes, like Satchmo about to blow the wierdest note on his trumpet. But all he said was:

'I've been here now some two years. The wife and the kids are also here.'

'When did you acquire the millstone?'

'She got pregnant. The old man would have nothing less than the confounded vowels at the altar,' he said. 'Now it's row after row though that, of course, is to be expected. After all, what's marriage all about? But it's getting me down. On the one hand I want to do the best thing for the child but I know and you'll agree that the best thing for any child in my vicinity is for me to disappear. I just can't get used to the reins. When you guys left the country I didn't know what to do with myself so I fucked off to Malawi; I couldn't make up my mind to go to West Germany or back to my final examinations. Glad I'm here anyway, if only because I am still in one piece. I would probably feel better if I had a grant and was reading something in the university here. Exile in London is so demoralizing. You're all changed. You all don't come on like you used to do back home. I mean everyone looks phoney and suspicious and cynical and there's no black feeling among us any more. You're all scraggy at the seams. And everyone seems to individualize themselves so much that even the sour comradeship that's still there really leaves a reek of sewage disposal systems. What's happened to us? What's happening to blacks here in London? We stand each to each like cities beyond repair. Shelley's Ozymandias has really come among us. Oh, I don't know. It's really good to see you. I thought you were dead or something. Lucky that, meeting you. I was at a loose end after work and thought I would buy Sterne's *Tristram Shandy*. I have a thing about that book. Would like to write like that. I am trying to do a novel but the hustle at the house with the wife is no fit climate remotely for anyone trying to write. She is a nurse. Yes, one of those. Seems to me all our black girls ever seem to do is to become nurses. I can't talk to her. She doesn't understand a single thing about art. Or books. Just blood and wounds and bedpans and screwing. What's happening to us? Just tell me that.'

I helped myself to another cigarette. So it had also happened to him. Behind every door lurks disillusionment; and he looked like one dazed by the kinds of interviews that always happen behind closed doors.

The long nights we had spent in his rooms arguing about the destiny of our country seemed now, five years later, remote, unreal, and as incredible as an alien planet. But there was one singular all-night session we had when we were frantically putting together material on Chaucer's *Troilus and Criseyde* which I still remember clearly. We could agree on nothing; indeed he and I then conducted ourselves like friends who on principle make everything a trial of strength, a contest. When morning came, we were still arguing and at breakfast we were silent and thoughtful because he and I were that day the ones to present papers at a two-hour seminar. But finally I told him that I knew enough about the thing to talk out the audience. When the time came and I stood up he winked so openly that everyone suspected something was up. But I kept a straight face and an hour and a half later sat down to tremendous applause. I still don't know how I did it. Confusion and disbelief had thrown the seminar into disarray. The remaining thirty minutes were quickly taken up by enthusiastic questions which I wearily parried—at that point I really was enjoying playing the role of the unfathomable black intellectual mind. I still do. But as soon as it was over I could no longer contain myself and we fled out on to the immaculate lawn where we tipped over in somersaults and overturnings, laughing so uncontrollably that passers-by stumbled in astonishment.

Now we were, five years later, sizing each other up to see if the kind of openness was no longer possible. Emigrés in a racially colour-conscious country, artificiality came quite easily to both of us. We were talking in English, feeling like hippopotami that have been doped with injections of English culture, and we were quite conscious of how we knew no useful skills besides blasé comments about the book world. Indeed, a new kind of decadence had caught up with us. Even the struggle for political independence had become no more than an articulate adze on which we could cut our milk teeth. We had come full circle, at once the circumference and the centre of ourselves, no longer knowing the poverty and degradation which had flung us up like waves from the masses of the sea. As I listened to him and to the inner unspoken discontent inside, I caught myself thinking how can we and the likes of us ever presume to lead the multitudes out there, thousands of miles away who day by day eke out a sordid existence, from the bullets and the toil and the bringing-up of children who will grow up to become just like us, sitting there in that Bloomsbury pub talking about the ennui that was like salt in our brains?

Whatever we did would always be scraggy at the seams. For, having wondered into the deep-end of the pool, we could only keep our heads above the water by continuing to keep our end up in the subjects and jobs we had chosen. But these were steeped with Graeco-Roman thinking which had nothing to do with the barren devastated townships we had come from. How easy it was to listen to the siren's promise of English pleasures! And how impossible to tear oneself away from that deadly embrace with its sweet bitterness and its endless provision for hours of self-recrimination and doubts. Out of the empty air Sisyphus comes down. Behind him Puck winks knowingly at us. At the rostrum, Cicero pauses to drink from the glass of water at his side. In the audience, Candide cannot find Cunegonde. The ale flows down our throats like communion wine from a wicked chalice.

'Just tell me that,' he repeated.

'I don't know how I've survived,' I said. 'But I know what you mean. It took me two years to realize that I was now totally on my own and could only pull myself up by my own bootstraps. I envy you being married, if only because she and the child are now people who are there for you even if now and then things are just row after row. I'm still a bachelor and a bad one at that. London is right at the edge where if you can't stand heights it's wiser not to look down at all. I lead a precarious existence, quite a penniless one and that makes it a little safer for me. Because I have always to keep the one thing I know how to do before me. At the same time accidents happen. One strikes lucky in the matter of friends who will keep a lookout if only because they know one is unwise and prone to recklessness. But too often my friends are just as reckless and on edge as I am and sometimes the burden of each other's needs is just too much and we load up our rucksacks and say goodbye without hard feelings. Just a sense of loss. My greatest disappointment has always been how one never gets the chance to give, and give unreservedly. So I do that in my writing, only interrupting the flow when the life of it gazes unseeing at the typewriter keys.'

He looked round. The pub was getting a bit crowded, stuffy, and it was the kind that I could see made him feel out of place because of its neatness and its phoney antiquity and its frequenters who were smart and white in every sense. It was enough to arouse the good old inferiority complex. I suggested that we go to the Marlborough. He agreed. The Marlborough was where most of the blacks in the vicinity usually went.

There we joined the one table where some black people I knew were sitting. I had found that however much I liked drinking on my own the surest way to attract attention and enmity was to enter a pub and directly join any blacks who may be there. That night we were all there, the people drawn together by the likeness of our skin and no more. The first time I had gone in there I had been struck by the way all our talk converged in a roundabout way to the insidious need for confirmation of one's status; we had each ferreted out each other's origins and then drank and talked of the cabbages and kings of racist phenomena and the onions and inkwells of the African image in diaspora. Though I lived quite near and had found the place by accident. In my wanderings I had met a group of white South Africans who lived up in Hampstead and at one of their frequent parties I had met a BBC researcher who had said that if I was lonely the Marlborough pub would straighten that problem out because it was 'okay'. Okay meant there was not much racism and there would be other blacks there. I had once made the mistake of going out alone in a district I did not know and into a pub I did not know and had, while walking home that midnight, been beaten up for my pains. I put that down to experience; it's never safe to presume that the English are not racist. But as we sat there in the safety of numbers and in the anonymity of educated talk which the beer was steadily stimulating, I could see how wretched our position was, always having to form a black laager against the hordes of the white natives. It was not enough for us to be black, proud and beautiful; little teeth of uneasiness always gnawed at our self-assurance for there is no answer to a whiteman's sneer. Hence the arguments, the fights, the violence. And hence the not invulnerable art of intellectual endeavour. And—once more the sneer. In other words, a circle, an impossible position, and the psychiatrist's couch.

The road had been so long and so arduous that it had sub-tracted us out of ourselves. The half-invisible phantasm that was left of us was what had gathered around our table. It was neither grim nor casual but restlessly leaping about in its own stillness, unable to be anything other than nervous and resentful and prone to a strange obsequious assertiveness. Examinations, lectures and tutorials were a kind of water-torture fashioned to test racial intelligence—and everything else seemed deliberately designed as an IQ test. Eysenck had really dug out the worms. But that humiliating paranoia somehow was transformed into a redeeming thing. It was like salt on a clean and open wound. Having built its existence on a denial of Victorian psycho-anthropology, on a denial of race and cultural inferiority, it could only sustain itself by continued denial. But how long would the provocation last? If it was suddenly withdrawn, someone would have to invent it again. The Christ-blood in the firmament had to be; and Faustus in his last hour had to be the one person alone to see it clearly streaming out of reach. And Mephistopheles certainly means to keep his appointment with us. In the meantime, the miraculous incision into the transparent waterskin of life holds our attention. And there are worthy excuses to explain the embarrassment—after all one is acquiring skills—much needed in the third world. Go, good countrymen, have yourselves a ball!

And indeed there was time to go to the Africa Centre that night where once more we felt safe and together and there was the prismatic effect of listening to a tall withered black South African talking about how Kaunda had returned to Smith a hundred and twenty-nine of our guerrillas in exchange for fifty million bags of maize and how also he had arrested SWAPO exiles and sent them to Nyerere who jailed them for ten years. But we all agreed that such things should not be publicized because it was in our interest to appear united. Afterwards, when the beer had settled in that tender spot in my deepest gut where I am one grim knot of pessimism, I looked around, at the bar where a few blacks in national costume were standing, at the dining tables where the smart black faces were eating impeccably African food recommended by the *Guardian*, and at the side seats where little groups of black and white faces sat talking and drinking in an unmistakeably non-racial way. Here then was the womb into which one could retreat to nibble at the warm fluids of an Africa that would never be anything other than artificial. A test-tube Africa in a brave new world of Bob Marley anguish, Motown soul, reggae disco cool, and the added incentive of reconceiving oneself in a friendly womb.

'Just tell me that,' he repeated.

The drink had intensified the catch in his throat. He had gone back in time to where we had been before. But this time he was looking at me as though he could not see me clearly and he looked like the usual walking discontent in search of a target. I looked back steadily at him. I did not particularly want an argument.

'Take it easy, man,' I whispered. But I could see that even this place had aroused in him that innate insecurity which had dogged him the whole evening.

When I had last known him he had been—whether drunk or not—immovable in temper; the kind of person whom you had literally to dynamite into losing his cool. But now he was staring at me in a smouldering questioning way. Looking at him I felt that things must be very bad: him with his wife and kid and his lack of sense of space and balance, where everybody else seemed to have mastered the art of maintaining poise. And here in the Africa Centre he was surrounded left and right by other blacks, all of whom seemed to be anything other than failures of disillusioned artists.

'You've become a hypocrite too,' he said.

He said it loud enough for the whole table to hear. I put down my drink and said wearily:

'If you say so.'

'I am saying so!'

I pointedly said nothing. But this was apparently a mistake for I realized that however blundering the attempt was he was seeking the kind of assurance which back in Africa he would never have needed to ask for. I had been like that once at Oxford and had not found the elixir but had tamed the need for it by a kind of bitter self-examination. He was a year older than I and he knew that I certainly expected him to be anything he chose to be as long as it did not put me into an impossible position. Like now.

'I'll get you a drink,' I said.

He bristled:

'You're not the only one with money, you know,' he sneered.

'Well, I'll get myself one.'

At the bar, a Nigerian journalist I know thumped me in the chest way of greeting.

'What's the situation, tonight?' he asked smiling, 'Drinking wine or beer?'

'Beer,' I said, feeling thankful about the friendliness. It always takes only a little unpleasantness to make me tense.

I returned to the table.

He had not cooled down. Jesus! It was going to be one of those nights. And the many times we had theorized together about how fights did not solve anything! And the many nights he had asserted that common sense and rational thinking should dictate behaviour! He had picked up my beer and was drinking it while looking steadily at me.

Though my gills ached at the provocation, I did not rise to the bait. Indeed, I think in a way I was feeling slightly smug about the way I was behaving correctly. This thing about behaving correctly and not according to the temperature of the blood was,

I think, what he meant by his accusation. I knew it the instant I rose to get myself another beer. After all, it was not every day I had money to buy a beer for a friend. He had seen that I was behaving like a European towards him. When I sat down again with the beer I smiled at him, wanting to tell him it was because I too was no longer sure about how to behave towards him after all these five years. But he said:

'I've heard all about you and your Oxford airs. You think I'm not good enough for you. You think I'm just an idiot dazed by the lights of London. You think you can put me in my place by acting the nabob on me. You think just because you're a writer you can use me as material for your stories. I know you though. Your brother was right about you. You're unbelievably selfish and vain and a fucking shit. I've heard all about you. You hate being black. If you could you would bleach yourself whiter than white. All these five years you never wrote back home. Do you know your uncle died a few months ago in a car crash? They told me how at a party in Hertford College, the people there said to you how sorry they were about it and you didn't even know what they were talking about! You're shit! All you think about is yourself all the time and using black people as material for your disgusting stories. You're filth, do you know that?'

He was almost shouting.

And then he leaned over and threw the rest of his beer into my face.

I half rose and froze in that position.

All conversation had ceased in the whole room. All eyes were fixed on me and they were all inscrutable. I had never looked at anyone so devouringly before and his eyes too were steady and cold and furious. It seemed an icy and merciless wire of eternity had suddenly sprung from the chill geography of living and struck deeply into the life inside me. The sudden blow of it straightened me up and I was standing over him for the first time, firmly on my own feet in that vast and anonymous London. Even my voice was as steady and warm as it could ever be: 'A pity to waste that beer. I'll get you another,' I said.

I picked up his glass and as I walked to the bar I could feel on the back of my neck the whole room breathing again. As I counted the coins—they were my last money from what I had got for selling my two review copies—I heard the conversations of the room picking up again. The girl behind the bar gave me a towel and I dried my face and hair. When I returned to the table, he was crying silently on to his shirtfront. I put the beer in front of him and sat down.

'Hey, Nyasha,' I called softly to him, 'get this down. It won't do you any good. But drink it all the same.'

He sat there rigid for a long moment. When finally he looked up his face was startlingly dry and the eyes were like diamonds newly cut. He reached out for the beer, nodded as though to someone millions of light years away, and drank deep.

I have not seen him since that fatal evening.

Otolith cupped the few fragments of biscuit and drawing back his head, palmed them into his mouth. I sipped at the cold and dead tea in my cup. People were now sunk deep in their chairs and cushions nibbling thoughtfully like self-conscious animal beings in an open field. Cicero and Liz were hard at it but I could sense that he was not making any headway. Liz was certainly some woman. Looking at her I could not make up my mind to ask about Helen. Perhaps it was better not to know. But I was uneasy because it was as if I was still trying to shield myself from unpleasant facts. Liz suddenly turned round and made an announcement:

'Listen, everybody. I have cleaned out the room at the end of the corridor to the right. It's a toilet. And it's now very much in working order. So we don't have to live like animals any longer. That's all.'

And she turned once more her whole attention to Cicero who still looked disconcerted by her sudden interruption of their argument. His bowler hat was now slightly askew and the shoulder knot of his toga was slipping down. The tic in the left half of his face was now so rapid it seemed that part of his face had been erased out of existence.

'Nothing exists but as it is perceived,' he insisted.

'That's Shelley,' Liz said smiling.

'For instance, children do not distinguish what they see and feel from themselves. Their nature is dissolved into the surrounding universe and the universe is absorbed into their being. And they have an unusual intense and vivid apprehension of life. Each is at once the point and the circumference; the point to which all things are referred, and the line in which all things are contained. Love—'

'But familiarity shields us from such tedious gazing, don't you think?' Liz asked unperturbed. 'All this unfathomable astonishment would put quite a strain on our eyes I should think. If life was really like that and all feeling and reason was simply the combined result of a multitude of impressions planted by reiteration, then we may as well pack up and close down our schools and universities,' she said.

'They are closed,' he said grimly.

'That's just this funny war. I did not learn linguistics and Old English from gazing at the smoky sky. The kind of reason I know is not learnt from gaping at scenery, neither does it grow on trees. And certainly the kind of feeling one "absorbs" from the Victoria Falls is not to be encouraged in anybody, let alone a child. I was once nearly eaten alive by a lion in the Serengeti Park. Though I was petrified I remember quite well what I felt looking at those great jaws and I know I did not like it. All this about intense and vivid apprehension of life is pure twaddle. One may as well learn one's alphabet from sewers as from water-colour scenery. It's no use building the creative "if" into one big system and labelling it The Romantic Image. There are too many loopholes in it. If you absorb too much of the sun you get sunburnt. If you absorb too much water you drown in it. If you absorb too much of the cold you freeze and get chillblains. If you absorb anything you better watch out it doesn't infect you with all sorts of diseases. It's all very well talking about reveries when a snake is crawling up your leg. But go on, Mr Cicero, I find you very interesting.'

Cicero hitched up his shoulder knot and steadied his wayward bowler. The dusky Latin glint in his right eye had long been declined and fallen in the Gibbon manner.

'Sterne says that if he was in the middle of a desert he would love some cypress,' he said heatedly. 'Surely this kind of power, this kind of want, makes us more than mere husks? The power to hear the music of a long-broken lyre and to see the fresh colours of the faded flower, surely this is more than mere empty phantasy? If the world is totally insensible to the urge and intuition in us, and I am not saying it is, then what inexhaustible melancholy shadows our every mood! There is such a thing as—'

'Be careful. Cold tea seems to have affected your brain for the worse. One of my students used to think that the description of the cross in the *Dream of the Rood* was like a police message about a jewellery robbery. And in *Pearl* too. There is such a thing as too much of a good thing, you know. However, I think I understand what you are trying to say. Your problem is that

70

you have not done your homework in linguistics, otherwise we would probably agree that "Nothing exists but as it is perceived" is one of those tricky little things linguistics and semantics rather than philosophy can solve. Wittgenstein probably dealt with it long ago. Anyway, it smacks of nonsense to insist on dogmatic pseudo-statements like that. Things are never as complicated as we feel. But they are not simply objects of thought. Or of feeling either. If everything in the world was an object of thought, think what a headache you would have right now. There wouldn't be enough aspirin, you know. I occasionally get attacks of migraine but that is probably because I lack iron or some such mineral. People who suffer from too great an appetite for open spaces like Wordsworth did can now be cured, you know. All this about absorbing the world into one is like Shelley's disbelief in the existence of distinct individual minds. He believed that "I" and "they" are not signs of any actual difference subsisting between people but are merely marks to denote the different modifications of the one mind; i.e., merely grammatical devices invented for arrangement, and totally devoid of the intense and exclusive sense usually attached to them. Had he lived longer perhaps he would have modified that. Your interest in drama is obviously along the same lines but people are people, human beings whom you can't dismiss as characters in search of a dramatist. I wouldn't like to belong to the same mind as a Nazi. One of my aunts died in Buchenwald. She wouldn't like it if I was to think that her personality was merely a grammatical device and part of the total mind which would have to include her concentration camp commandant. I don't think you are at all part of the one mind with those sort of racists we used to have a lot of trouble with on the campus.'

Cicero gazed round him in a vague and dazed manner. He was like a boxer whom Muhammad Ali had just about annihilated. Norman Mailer would probably have relished the fight from a nearby armoured glass cage. But Cicero did not know when he was losing:

'But the essential attribute of poetry is that it has the power of awakening in others sensations like those which animate the poet. Painting and music also have the same quality, music especially with its transcendental significance. Is it not because they have some intelligible and beautiful analogy with the sources of emotion and thought? The desire to awaken in all things a community with what we experience within ourselves is not a phantasy but a reality. We call it love. There is a spirit within me at enmity with nothingness and dissolution. It seeks a bond with man and with everything which exists.'

'Look out of the window and you'll see the answer to that,' she said.

Cicero blinked, dipping his head slightly. And then he drew himself upright like one about to tread unshod upon the unreasonable world. I passed my eye over the room. In the far corner sat one who looked smilingly at everything that passed. He was dressed in an old and tattered dressing gown that had certainly survived the rigours of the better part of the War. It looked like the kind of hardy trench-coat which would see a timid man through the missiles and bombs of dreams. At the same time it was like the one which Dostoevsky invented as the uniform of characters constipated by ennui and wretchedly cursed with manservants of insolent wit. The face was as long as it was broad; its outstanding feature was its unremarkability: two wide-apart beady eyes, a miserably crestfallen negro nose, and a mouth perpetually stretched into smiling by a vacant and unnatural void that glowed luminously beneath the dark skin. Here then was an African Schweik. He caught my eye and nodded self-consciously. I walked over and sat on the arm of his chair.

He said, in greeting:

'Dreadful world, isn't it?'

'What?'

'I said dreadful world, isn't it?' he said.

I agreed. He took a deep breath and added casually,

'Anonymous lanes where misery treads unkown through the fog with cries as silent as pennies in the nether belly of a jukebox. Here none scrutinizes the crescent moon but through a mist of desolation whose only sound drills into the skull phantasma of black multitudes sorrowing. The newly-born are condemned to seek unborn routes and wander through the pulsing cloudbreak toward the secret horror of the storm where old and cynical gods still dream where last they dreamed and fell in the darkened byways of tradition-tried hell. In the schoolroom marking their books I glean from my pupils' essays the disease soon to overtake their minds and plunge them hysterically strait-jacketed into the abattoir world of guns and meat-cleavers.'

I had taken off my spectacles to clean them but his words arrested my hands and I just stared short-sightedly at him. The two beady eyes were like needles about to strike at a point midway between my eyes. He was still smiling but the smile was like the sound of a cat mournfully crying its sorrows in the dark of a rickety staircase. He continued:

'Each time I see beautiful flowers their ugliness inside me thrusts out its two hands twitching to tear the white world out of them. In time I see photographs of nude black women their rage inside me hurling out its bile, burning to seize and shake the white world out of us. But the void inside me extrudes the entrails of hollow endeavour soon to madden them too. And I drink hungrily some nights the bitter alcohol of guilt underlying every achievement until the midnight shadows extend their tentacles into my headache of a brain. When I wake up in some woman's bed, the future before me like a nightmare of slick cliches; the hangover inside me like a culture that's truly dead. And I stand by the sink in the tiny kitchen watching the sad aurora glare above the linchen. A drowsiness erases the bitterness from the bitter words. The other side of the world is a single drop of blood away. The few steps to the door are the feelings vanished from the room. What there ever was of you and me is a film of dust that's easily swept away. But this skin of watery dusk enfolds you with flames of memories where there is no silence when sound ceases. The sunlight in a glass of cold water makes the world softer. And what my face cannot express holds my gaze when death unveils. It is the dark and calm in the whirlwind's iron palm where broken hearts are wrecked and driftwood cast on sandbank outgrains the texture of human moment. An empty house on an empty earth creaked beneath the prodigal's feet. Only the land that's framed by the empty blue sky is enclosed like a brain in my skull. The dust that will reclaim me fashioned me; it falls like snowflakes upon everything in my life. When I stand still and look through the pitch dark of myself, I reach out for the electricity switch which is not there. I have to grope my way blindly to the creaking stairs into the innermost memory where I am awake screaming at the sudden lights between a woman's thighs. That silent house is full of fantasy; that emptied heart is a hollow dream. The vain luminous hills glow with indifference; the clear blue sky, big and round, vibrates with hopeless oracles. All I had to lose were years of loneliness; the long nights and days I spent with me. I am only complete when I feel something's missing; something unattainable, like a purpose, a design. But I go crazy sometimes wondering what the hell! I get mad, I guess, thinking what a fucking thought!

'That's when the chill from beyond fades into warm doorways and crams descriptions of Africa into a confined room. That's when the rain out of the empty air pulls down a victim tense and white. What is it pounding at my door like brain and tongue red-hot to speak? The fist is clenched around Golgotha-red flowers to crack the stony heart with hammers of human knuckles. Not a shred of emotion lingers; the wind has scoured it all. A frail and tattered grace outlines the continent in the round moonlight. Oh, black insider! We should have turned at that corner where the crucified man pointed the way. At that corner where Chaka washed his hands in blood. At that corner where the road to Kampala leads to Buchenwald. At that corner where black learned men in disgrace sink their differences with the rest. But we will drive through to the independent countries where lucid minds shatter through thick windscreens. Where original thoughts veer and crash into ancient lamp-posts. Where promising youths are driven to drink cynical toasts while you and I clap with one hand the praises of the human traffic. We should have gone the other way; with Hieronymus Bosch scrawled massacre nightmares on the Coca-Cola billboards; with Dylan Thomas written states of mind that crack mountains; with Soyinka drawn typewritten portraits of madness rooted in sanity in the Africa hereafter. I should have turned at that corner where history moulders in grimy basement rooms. Because the blow to my jaw did not solve his problem. I sat there, eyes open, seeing nothing. The kick to my head did not solve his problem. He broke the chair on my shoulders and stood back to observe how even this did not solve anything. Not once had I moved toward the savage penitence which would have released both of us from the crude scenario. I had been beaten up before for not behaving like people wanted me to, especially not expressing appreciation or gratitude and had sat there, eyes open, seeing nothing.

'At last he called the others and they sat in a circle around me to discuss democratically what was wrong with me. Soon it was my turn to speak. But even as I began to say "There is nothing inside me wrong with me" their faces lengthened in disgust until finally he spat out his cigarette shouting: "Can't you see you can't reject everything and everybody?" Once more the blows and kicks; and the chair smashing my shoulders were all helping them into a frenzy upon me who had never asked help of them. I tell you, insider, the hills of Africa are red with wounds from long ago. A sorrow of atoms spins us unaware through void and limit to abandon us to the icy tumult from beyond. There on the outermost edge of sense, Africa weeps. There are no tears on her grief-wrung cheeks but a sudden ageing shrinking inward her soul and mouth tightening about the skull into hills. How should I know, insider! Only that as dawn breaks a bare knee from where I sleep, I ponder every day where I should stay; whether, solidly in my own mind or in the real Africa of give and take. To burn incense at the shrine of dread seems at best, after the bitter pilgrimage, the activity of an insane sanity. But to play their game to the grimy end of definitions and counter-definitions of Africanness requires a zest and stamina I do not have. Only one path remains, insider, through the hardy water of faceless oases toward the harsh and arid aurora where love and hope are dimmed only to their unrefusing core.'

He paused. There was an unyielding glint in his eyes. My bottom had fallen asleep and I stood up to stretch it awake. As I did so, I caught the amused crinkle that enclosed his vacant smile.

'Do you write poetry?' I asked him.

He looked at me oddly.

'I used to; now I just talk.'

'What did you mean by "insider"?'

His fingers drummed impatienty on the arm of the chair. He muttered:

'Does it matter? Inside-out is outside-in, but there's always bleeding. And hidden persuaders. Do you know how to make a man who walks away from his shadow? It is an illusion based on chemical preparation. A screen having the appearance of an ordinary white blind is shown. The performer stands behind this screen while the stage or room lights are turned off; a strong light behind him causes his shadow to appear on the screen; while he moves freely about, the shadow moves accordingly. No matter what position he takes, the shadow still appears on the screen; if he walks away from the screen, the shadow remains fixed, visible to the audience. Then the stage lights are turned on, the shadow vanishes. This can be repeated several times, the performer each time assuming a different position. The explanation is this: the screen is coated or sprayed on the side away from the spectators with luminous green paint. The light used has a colour attachment consisting of a film or strip of gelatine preferably on a wheel painted red, green and blue. An assistant turns the wheel, so as to bring first the red portion of the gelatine strip before the light which will make the light show red. The performer can move freely about because the red light does not affect the luminous material on the screen. Next, have the assistant turn the wheel for the green colour and assume the position the shadow of which you wish to appear on the screen. Then have the wheel turned so that the light will show blue and, after you have kept your position in the blue light for a few seconds, walk away from your shadow, coming in front of the screen. The best method of carrying out the trick is first to station the assistant at the light; then tell the audience that you have the power to separate yourself from your shadow. Simply step behind the screen, between the light and the screen and call out "Red!". The assistant immediately turns the wheel to bring the red part of the gelatine strip before the light. After a few seconds, call out "Green!". The assistant then turns on the green light. Stand a few seconds in the position you wish to cast on the screen, the green light having little effect on the luminous material. Still holding the same position call out "Blue!". The assistant immediately turns the wheel to bring the blue portion of the strip on the light. Lastly, call out "Green!". This time the assistant turns the wheel to bring before the light a part of the gelatine strip that has been rendered opaque; this shuts off the light. The performer then walks away from the screen. The onlookers will get the impression that there is a green light on, because the screen itself glows green, due to the luminous material with which it was sprayed before the exhibition. You see? The insider walks away from his shadow.'

'I have a little shadow that goes in and out with me. What can be the use of him is more than I can see,' I said.

'Subtract a man from himself and all you've got is just a shadow,' he said looking pointedly at me. 'Chip away at the marble, down to the substance that holds the core together. There, we are mere abstractions. Ephemeral Macbeth travelled in that region. Caligula too. It is the inwardness of a candle which a mere breath can put out. When a man crossing a bridge meets himself going the other way, the void beckons him to follow. The ability to walk away from your own shadow, to walk away from the evidence of one's own existence, is at the source of dreams, ghosts, myths, spirits. In this room, each one has his own way of doing it. It's not so much that every man is not an island as what intercourse can two heaps of putrid clay and crumbling bones hold together? The organs of sense are destroyed, the eyes eaten out, the heart black and without emotion, the intellect perished. It is in the corpse at our feet that we see the evidence of our own destiny. What would I not give to be able to walk away from it! Shelley said when you can discover where the fresh colours of the faded flower abide, or the music of the broken lyre, seek life among the dead. I only know that where there is death, where there is pain and despair, or just mere nothingness, there you find a maximum of silence and a minimum of words. The same is the case where sub-surface feelings and thoughts express themselves against our wishes. Faulkner's *The Sound and the Fury* in the first part articulated the autistic world of one for whom the external world was an extension of the sources of feeling and thought. At the same time a surfeit of words, where there are two worlds of life and death, interrupted by intolerable and tenuous silences, creates within us a malediction, nausea. The image leaps out of the mirror to take over the mask and surface of our lives. Most never notice it's happening to them. Some welcome it. I yield room big enough for us to coexist without obvious antagonism. In that way I am two people; others are more. You look to me like one of those who turn a blind eye to their own self-evident existence.'

'Self-effacement is an art I have not yet mastered,' I said.

'That's not what I meant,' he mumbled. 'I travelled widely in Europe before I came back home. The expense was not worth it but I would not have missed the experience for anything. I do not know why we have to go through bitter experience to discover simple truths that have always been right there underneath our nose. Love is not as daunting and frightful a commitment as I had thought. Neither is it a sordid and casual complication which one forgets in the heat of day-to-day duties. It's human beings. It's us. When it dies, then there is no hope for us. Nothing. I don't know exactly how I learnt that. I was terribly lonely, especially in England where every day the newspapers carried the most hysterical nonsense about blacks and Asians. I had never really come to terms, I suppose, with my blackness—I had never particularly noticed that I was black—and it was something of a shock suddenly to realize that my skin for the English was a natural label that read Mugger, Rapist, Amin, Inferior. That kind of thing. But when I read about blacks being beaten up by the National Front and by the police who were also attacking black business premises, I could not believe that the same thing would happen to me. I was too bound up in my books. I had just handed in my thesis and decided to go out for a drink to unwind. I knew a nice pub which was very difficult to find; you had to go through a series of alleys. There I drank and smoked and drank.

'At closing time I was the last to leave. There was a full moon. It made everything stark and clear-cut. One of those lucid thoughtful nights when it's easy to imagine things. But I had not imagined the man who blocked the alley and had a knife in his hand. I had not seen him until I was within a yard of him. His breath reeked of whisky. And he was grinning. The hairs stood on end at the back of my head. I had never fought anybody. At the same time I had never been stuck up with a knife. The thing was ludicrous enough to be real. He made a movement and in that instant I felt the blade dig into my side. It exploded inside my head that this was a ridiculous way to go. That's what saved me. I went berserk. The next thing I knew policemen were dragging me from the wretched man who was unconscious in my hands. They had started to beat me up when I passed out. I woke up in hospital to find myself under guard and charged with grievous bodily harm and intent to commit robbery. There were alternative charges of being drunk and disorderly.

'I could think nothing but wild thoughts of what was happening to me. The first time I realized I was in the hands of whitemen and their kind of law. I could not even begin to admit to myself that I would receive any kind of justice. I had visions of a statement being issued that I had thrown myself from a window or strung myself up in a toilet or somehow killed myself. I did not know any lawyers. It suddenly struck me that everybody I knew was white. My own colleagues, right down to the nurses in the hospital. It paralysed a part of me, realizing that I was on an island that contained millions of whites who were all suddenly personally against me. I could only think of trying to escape. It was so unreal it had to be real. That's why the memories came. I remembered my parents who had always taken care of everything for me. I could have murdered somebody at that moment. I could have stood up at that moment shouting Guilty! Guilty! I could have jumped out of the window. But all I did was to ask to make a phone-call to Professor Outlaw who was the head of the Law Faculty. I told him all that had happened. He was furious. He came over right away. It was just after midnight. And then he went off muttering something about a sick society. Minutes later I was told I was free.

'I never quite knew what really happened but Outlaw had a long reach. Life is thickly knit with this kind of grit but I would prefer it not to be mixed into my porridge. I never could stand sand in my food. But that is not what I meant. I merely wanted to say that, however much one may live solely in the design of one's own mind, there are millions out there who also have designs. Reducing you to a mere abstraction on a hate poster. Or just a shadow lurking among their fears. Vibes. Bad vibes, good vibes; they are there in the wind like magnetic fields affecting every little act of kindness or horror. It's then glorified into some kind of moral or principle which is a good way of putting a man in the right, in the wrong. Like colonialism, that great principle which put anyone who was not white in the wrong. Create education and immediately you put others into a false position of inferiority. Equate whiteness with good and, of course, blackness becomes always tainted. A glance at the index of a thesaurus tells you exactly how blackness is equated with funereal, bad, dirty, prohibited, odium, condemnation, shame, defame, ruffian, sorcery, offender. Comedians make the most of what they can with words like blackleg, black-out, blackmail, black magic, black cap. And we have assimilated the language and are teaching it to our children. Think of the psychological snarl-ups!'

'I suppose,' I said, 'we are it. But it does not have to be inevitable. Our own language does have the same associations. But the thing about becoming shadows rings true. Becoming attitudes; becoming all surface, with no depth underneath. At the same time, why stress depth, or rootedness for that matter. We are a continent of refugees; one day here, another day there; so much fodder for the boundary makers. There is no sense of home any more, no feeling of being at one with any specific portion of the earth. As you said we have to seek unborn routes and these, like the evidence of ourselves, are yet to come. We live as though we were rehearsing our roles in a misty womb where we cannot see the text clearly but as it were remember vaguely the general theme of it. Which is everything to do with the history of this continent. A continent of wounds which no longer knows what it is to be whole and healthy. A country disfigured by scars and broken teeth and smashed testicles can only writhe in nightmare over and over, reliving the horrors that started it all. A village milked of its youth and left to fester on a hill, inhabited only by the old and lame, can only bask in the sun, waiting for death. These new towns crowded with thousands of homeless unemployed whose dreams are rotting in the gutters, are only the new dunghills from which will emerge iron flies in a cloud to scatter all over the hills.

'At the same time, human life has lost its old sanctity and is snuffed out at the drop of a new cause. The corpses that litter the streets out there no longer make anyone pause to reflect on what you call destiny; they are just so much rotting meat to be stepped over on our way to another looting. When I was sixteen, seventeen, I began writing bits and pieces of the prose-poem kind about such imaginary things as Mother Africa, Black Woman, and the kind of intensely romanticized Africa which could only exist in a pride-starved adolescent. The black-is-beautiful kind of thing. Like Langston Hughes, Leroi Jones, Senghor, and the negritude school. At the same time I was getting into D. H. Lawrence, trying I suppose to find some meaningful pattern to the changes taking place then inside me. The thing I remember most about it is that I always tried to reduce everything into a sort of autobiographical record. As though I needed to stamp myself with the evidence of my own existence; as if every single thing I did and said was pregnant with significance. Every transient emotion was the occasion for poetry. Every passing spectacle an epiphany. States of mind in their instantaneity were biographies, autobiographies of the whole continent. I think this was the one significant effect of the black literary renaissance as it was called from Harlem to Ibadan. Suddenly it seemed all our best minds were accessible, had experienced the same anguish as ourselves, had felt the same anger and humiliation at the hands of whites and were writing about it to let every brother know. And then, of course, it turned out that the African image which we ourselves were constructing in our novels and poems was as limited and as false as in the white novelists' and poets' descriptions. Perhaps the limitation and falseness are inbuilt within the novel as a genre which has—with few exceptions such as *War and Peace*—never fully accommodated the multitude and psyche of whole continents. At the same time the forces that gave rise to the black renaissance in letters were the specific and immediate demands for independence and historical purity. Such forces were peculiarly fertile in the fashioning out of the epic style of novel such as Achebe's *Things Fall Apart* and Ngugi's *A Grain of Wheat*. I must confess though that I grew up on Peter Abraham's *A Wreath For Udomo* in which the roots of our history and the possibility of an African image were explored, as in the other two.

'The connection between what is happening inside us and what is happening outside us in the Africa without had been made. At the same time the seeds of disillusion were sown: Okonkwo's alienation from his own shadow and his subsequent suicide; Ngugi's awareness of the betrayal of *uhuru*; and Abraham's prophetic insight into the sort of corrupt expediency which an African frontline state can get into. But there was one weakness in all this: history is not something standing outside and apart from us; it is human beings. It is as much Okonkwo as it is the administrator. That both are inflexibly human, or are not, is the complex pathos of the tragedy. Yet neither of them is able to walk away from his own shadow; indeed their shadows are bigger than themselves and are presented as that history necessity which is supposed to stand apart in the world outside the sources of thought and feeling. Such historical walls are always spattered with the blood of minds that have smashed themselves to bits there. The idea of personality moulded by the cultural artifacts outside us and the sense of identity with a specific time and place, as though the human being is as rooted in his own kind of soil as any weed, is what creates for us the emperor's new clothes. And it is quite easy inflexibly to deceive ourselves that we are fully clothed and not naked.

'The psychology of clothes has much to do with notions of history and identity. Alex Haley now has a full wardrobe of roots. In the *Iliad*, the Greeks and the Trojans were all at pains to clothe themselves with armour of rhetoric, with gods and goddesses, with attitudes and values, with gore and law, with guts and poetry, with ceremony and acrimony, with ideals and the realism of victory. It is as if the Trojan War clothed the Greeks with the apparel of nationhood. It was therefore fitting that the *Odyssey* should find Ulysses's wife surrounded by suitors, each one of whom wanted to get the privilege of undressing her. The bloody battle at the end becomes heroic when the husband, in defending and asserting his conjugal rights—she had kept the suitors at bay by weaving cloth—defends and asserts the honour of his state. We therefore have in Homer a vision of the nakedness of the Greeks whose new clothes they display so effectively to the Trojans and to the reader. And it all begins with the question of who is undressing Helen. Not only is the naked flesh open to temptation but it is also vulnerable to the sword; hence manhood, strength, honour even, is the magnificence (or lack of it) of one's armour. Defeat does not mean loss of face but loss of one's armour to the victor.

All this applied also to the expression or masking of feelings; the war as an emergency demanded unity of effort, the submergence of individual images within the one mass of the national army. But the kind of hero image with which the Greeks had always clothed their minds and the minds of gods with which they had always dressed their imagination were both unsuited to the sorts of unity the war demanded. Achilles sulks; the gods dispute among themselves. Agammemnon is too inflexible and Menelaus too ridiculous. In short, Homer does, as it were, a strip-tease of the ancient Greeks.

'Here history is not something outside man, but man in his own merciless nakedness, in spite of the emperor's new clothes. Aye Kwei Armah in his *The Beautiful Ones Are Not Yet Born* not only stripped the African image of its clothes but also forced it to undergo a baptism of shit. Okigbo's inexorable resculpting of our nakedness in the Pygmalion sense filled his homecoming with shadows of the conflict that would kill him. And Gabriel Okara, with his ear to its heartbeat, listened to the inner voice that was being stifled by the new style and by the unheeded crumbling of the old historical walls. The voice penetrates to the innermost promptings of human accessibility which can find no meaning except brutal response in the man-made artifacts surrounding it. Here a chasm is exposed within the African image; our roots have become so many banners in the wind, with no meaningful connection with the deep-seated voice within us. But they have at the same time strengthened their grip on us: a new kind of fascism based on the "traditional" African image has arisen. Ngugi is in jail, eating his grain of wheat. And here we are drinking tea in the rabble of the war.'

I paused, looking out through the window. The sun was hidden behind thin trails of cloud through which its white-hot rays penetrated down to the smoking ruins of the city. In the remote distance I could see what looked like parachutes drifting down to the earth. Something deep inside me tightened into a knot of pain. So, this too was a poem by a doctor somewhere in the Gambia. Progress.

'The world out there and the world in here,' he said, 'made each other. They will soon come for us, whoever they are. There will be no words then, just a ghastly butchered silence, like everywhere else. Of course, we mean nobody any harm but that has always been exactly why people like us end up dead. We are an affront to them; their strength has always been aware of the pathos of the weak.'

'Lenrie Peters!' I exclaimed irrelevantly. 'Those parachutes coming down. Had Adam fallen like that perhaps the world outside Eden would not be so bad after all.'

He scratched his collarbone like one who is about to be garrotted.

'This faculty is a refuge, an Eden,' he said. 'That's why it will not last. An artificial Eden. I spent years unable to survive the grim give and take, bribe and rule, world out there. I missed the campus atmosphere of earnest and innocent inquiry. I like books, not lean and hungry looks. At the same time I was appalled at how it has become more and more difficult to change for the better the lives of our people. My best intentions were simply the evidence of my failure. So I spun a cocoon of intricate dilemmas around myself and went to sleep at the heart of them in this faculty. That bomb on the roof is a neat irony. We have, so to speak, all the ingredients of a philosophical farce. Remember the Dinner at Trilmachio's? I would not have missed it for anything. It's exactly what goes on in the houses of our great and rich right here in Africa. Meanwhile it's still all for the best, even if "six dethroned kings having supper together at an inn was a sight never seen or heard of before".[13] Here there is not the restraint of good intentions or bad feeling on any parts. There is neither surprise nor astonishment. There are no do-gooders to convict one, nor politicos to harangue us for votes. One is utterly naked, or as much as one cares to be. I have always admired Dostoevsky's dressing gowns and overcoats. Hence I am wearing this and exploring our notes from underground. Yes, I am writing a little tract which perhaps you'd care to have for I'll have no use for it, except to light my pipe.

'Literacy is the surgeon's needle with which I bind my wounds. I would do a better job of it if I had an anaesthetic. I suffer from insomnia. And wear Gogol's overcoat at nights and seek out the secret of his genius. Africa needs him desperately, otherwise we will choke in self-disgust. I have found in nineteenth-century Russian literature an empathy with the breath and experience of Africa which I have not found in literature. And yet we write as though Pushkin, Turgenev, Gogol, Tolstoy, Chekov, Lermontov had never existed. It's not that I am saying we should imitate them as that we should at

13. 'Dinner at Trimalchio's' is part of Petronius' *Satyricon*, written in Latin around Emperor Nero's time, first published in 1660.

least know what has been done and where possible build upon that. Life is not a plot, you know. It does not have one coherent theme but many conflicting ones. But, thank God, it does have a beginning and an unequivocal end. To sustain itself all it needs is to be continuously reminded in simple unremembered kindness that all the old lessons about love are true. If I was stranded in a desert I would not love a cypress but dream of another human being. Probably some woman from my life, or from all the horde of fictional characters whom all writers have invented up to this day. That's a lot of human beings, and a lot of imagined ones too. Anyway I would probably be too thirsty to agree with John Donne's "no man is an island".[14] If it tolls for thee, how come all the German citizens turned a blind eye to the millions who were being gassed and roasted among them. All their clothes and banners were flying and they couldn't see the concentration camp in the mirror; all their philosophical, musical, and literary underpants were flying and they couldn't see exactly what they were doing to a Jew's testicles.

'We now do the same thing; we raise the African image to fly in the face of the wind and cannot see the actually living blacks having their heads smashed open with hammers in Kampala. We have done such a good advertising and public relations stunt with our African image that all horrors committed under its lips merely reinforce our admiration for the new clothes we acquired with independence. And, of course, the horrors are themselves one more reason to tighten the screw of our peculiar brand of fascism. For a people seeking freedom we are much practised in intolerance among ourselves. And I don't just mean the tribal syndrome. I've burnt my fingers too many times on it to dismiss it off-hand. It's the way we not only adapted very easily to the materialism of the West but also quite deliberately inherited their kind of social class distinctions whereby a man's worth is measured by his wallet and his educational certi-ficates—and this penny-certificate elite has been ruling Africa since so-called independence was granted, especially where military coups have not happened for the military coup was the response of the uneducated. Meanwhile we silence the press, the trade unions, the opposition, the student unions, and all societies which may become the focus of intelligent dissent. All this for the sake of the African image which is no longer worth the snot it quotes.'

He laughed and sipped at his empty cup.

14. John Donne, *Devotions* (1624), XVII.

'An excessive indulgence of the senses and thoughts,' he continued, 'leads to the kind of decadence which can paralyse all action. To tick all the orifices of pleasure and stimulate all the possible orgasms of intellectual heights would be the sort of contrast demanded by this sordid war. But now that we attain erections by disembowelling the weak and by torturing the obdurate, and ejaculate at the sight of cringing humanity, what, I ask you, is the end of it all? We have rapidly armed ourselves to the teeth with the outward trappings of national advancement, as though by surrounding ourselves with these outward signs of social and national coherence we can will into our innermost craving the same edifices of peace and order. It is a Tower of Babel that can reach the moon. Zaire has leased itself out to German nuclear tests; is bringing in Foreign Legionnaires to squash the lives of its poor. The Organization of African Unity has become the maintenance man of the black ancient regimes and not the instigator and protector of the people's liberties. Amin's atrocities have made all the other atrocities elsewhere respectable. What could not have brought the crises more in perspective than that Bokassa should conceive the original idea of crowning himself emperor in the Napoleonic style? Mongo Beti's story of the old man and the medal had clearly come home to roost. Petronius would feel quite at home there—until of course his own veins are opened. Our search for freedom has not included the most elementary humanitarian justice such as the abolition of the death penalty or better care for the mentally sick or homes for the elderly. It's still as much every man for himself as it ever was.'

'But Tanzania—'

He made a very rude gesture.

'If you knew all, you'd know there are no buts,' he said. 'If it was for this war you wouldn't be able to write what you are writing. We would not even be able to live like this. We'd probably be in some field doing the hoeing of the revolution. Or in a camp learning to respect whatever ideology came into their minds. Or, more simply, we'd be dead. We are no good to both sides. The mark of the plague cannot protect us forever. Christ! I've made myself quite ill thinking about the world out there. I don't think we have any guns here to defend ourselves.'

Liz shouted from across the room:

'Yes, we have. I brought as many as I could find out there. Anyone who has nothing against it may help themselves to one. It's the ammunition that's the trouble. I just brought everything mixed up. We'll probably have to experiment before we find out which bullets fit what gun. But it is quite all right now.'

Cicero was appalled:

'You've brought guns in here?'

'Yes, isn't it splendid?' Liz said smiling.

'GUNS!'

'What's the matter with you?' she demanded calmly.

'Mother-fucking warmongering shit! Do you realize what you have done?'

'I've given us the means to defend ourselves if ever the need arises.'

'Fucking Christ!'

'For a pacifist, you have a most warlike and mercenary vocabulary.'

'Ợ%§$X/£?!'

'I didn't catch that,' she said.

He could not hold her gaze.

An alarm bell startled us by suddenly beginning to ring from nearby. The conversation stopped for only a fraction of a second. When I looked out I could still see hundreds of parachutes floating down to the ground.

I asked Liz:

'Do you know who they are?'

She indicated the binoculars on the coffee table.

'Their planes do not have any markings. They could be anybody.'

Cicero came out of his sulk.

'Can't we talk about something else? This faculty is no house of war. For who maketh thee to differ from another? And what hast thou that thou didst not receive? Now if thou didst receive it, why dost thou glory, as if thou hadst not received it?'[15]

And from the equipoise of the deep, Otolith assented:

'Amen. And yet if a woman who is a carrier for a colour-blind factor marries a man with normal colour vision, any sons born to such a marriage would have only a fifty-fifty chance of having normal colour vision. The old Greek philosopher said "Everything flows." And Sophocles could only mumble "These things are not of today or yesterday, but of all times, and no man knows when they appeared." Heredity supplies the raw material which the influence of the environment moulds into the individual. Colour-blindness, haemophilia, diabetes can be

15. St Paul's First Epistle to the Corinthians, 4, 7.

inherited. Atavistic characters can go back for hundreds of generations to some ancestral form such as human infants born with rudimentary tails. The other human recessives are the morons who sometimes do not exceed the mental capability of a normal child of four or five, while others may reach mental ages of twelve or thirteen. Their mental deficiency is not due to lack of education but to the absence of a capability of being educated. And no amount of education will take the mental defective beyond a certain point. The high-grade morons eke out an existence as the lowest grade of unskilled workers and they form a slum population which they continually increase because of their unthinking fecundity. A biologist says that such families are a product of civilization, because under natural selection they would not survive to carry on their race. 'Mendel's experiments told him among other things that a tall sperm may fertilize a tall egg to give rise to a pure tall plant, a pure dominant; and a dwarf sperm may fertilize a dwarf egg to give rise to a pure recessive dwarf plant. Now apply this little song to people and see if you can talk about free-will or individuality. However there was Lamarck: fortunately his law of use and disuse and the inheritance of acquired characteristics all stress the direct effect of the environment in modifying organisms such as us born black in a white environment. I have always felt sorry for the dinosaur whose special modifications, when the climate changed from wet to dry, made them unable to fit in with the new dry and arid conditions and they became extinct. You could say the same thing happened to the Tasmanians who could not adapt to the brutal and murderous presence of English whites. However the law of recapitulation perhaps consoles you, Cicero, in that your very own individual development repeats the principal stages in evolutionary history. Maybe that's what you see in Christ.'

Cicero straightened his bowler, refusing to be put in his place:

'Where are the good old ancient times when men believed in spontaneous generation as did Virgil in his account of the production of bees. And the Egyptians who believed that crocodiles could be formed in the Nile mud. And until the time of Pasteur, Europe's belief that maggots' bacteria can be produced by decomposition. Where is the peace and quiet of Eden with its special creation, in which we were invented at the beginning of time with the same physical structures as we have now—apart from a matter of losing our virginity? No wonder there's war here. No wonder we are fucked up like this. Our actions, I suppose, are not our fault but that of our genes and environment.

There is no romance in that kind of mathematics but a cold and chilling engineering which would deny us uniqueness, unless we are merely as unique as a random number. The same sort of disillusionment came with Copernicus' refutation of Ptolemy's statement that "the earth lies right in the middle of the heavens." Martin Luther could only exclaim "The fool wants to turn the whole world upside down." And that was just the beginning. Galileo toyed with the first telescope, discovering the mountains on the moon, the phases of Venus and the four little stars attending Jupiter, and observed that the sun rotates. Kepler, observing the planets, discovered that they move not in a circle but in ellipses. Newton determined the basic principles of light and colour, created integral and differential calculus, and defined the working of gravity. He formulated the laws of motion, determined the moon's effect on the tides, made the first reflecting telescopes, and discovered that a prism separates light into component colours. His epitaph reads "Mortals, congratulate yourselves that so great a man has lived for the honour of the human race." That's a bit steep, I guess. Meanwhile the skies were being observed to distraction by Herschel who discovered Uranus and found proof that Newton's law of gravitation applied outside the solar system and discovered the path the sun follows through space carrying the planets with it. Suddenly it was 1919, and gravitation was found to bend light. Motion, time, and distance were not absolute but relative moving frames of reference. $E = mc^2$. The atom bomb had come. Do you see what I mean? How we have been inexorably put on a path of more menacing discoveries. We are denied the security of a medieval ignorance and have to live under the shadow of the bomb. And since Hubble tampered with it the universe has started to explode wildly outward, with each more distant galaxy hurtling away at proportionately greater speed. I was the first of my line to go to school and learn this. After a time I just couldn't understand my people and they couldn't understand me. They were talking in terms of the cosmogonies of a special creation as in Achebe's *Arrow of God* and I was talking in terms of genes and chromosomes, and calculus and relativity and the new astronomy. At first they tried to beat me up into submission but I fucked off out of there to try to do drama and have been trying ever since. It's not of a life I lead but at least it does not preclude simple and direct feelings for fellow humans.'

Liz coughed:

'You are neither simple nor direct, Cicero. I find you complex and roundabout. But if you mean the instincts, then you ought to know that instincts are also not simple or direct. Rather they are shrouded in secrecy. But of course there is the simplicity and directness of an immature intellect or of an idiotic temperament. Hamlet sometimes used too well this latter kind of simplicity to very great effect with the aid, of course, of an antic disposition. The calculated idiocy of a Machiavellian prince is, of course, more interesting than the sentiments of a generation brought up on nothing but ready-made phrases about war and peace, about ecology and health foods, about nation-making and health. I wish, Cicero, you would say something really original about war rather than just fuck it out of court. Did you do *Lysistrata*?'

Cicero at once brightened up:

'That was my favourite! A great play that, and so modern too. It could beat *Hair* any time. I mean *Hair* was really scraping the bottom of the musical barrel and coming up with masturbation, fellatio, etc. I've nothing against masturbation, I do it all the time. I did like the live performance more than the record. But *Lysistrata*! Shit. A class of its kind. I mean, how else can one treat sex dramatically? That play has it all. If it was ever produced by Playboy Productions we would probably wake up to find our hair turned completely white. It's got everything in it: sex equality, sex war, sex diplomacy, etc. The bedroom is brought right out into the open. Of course, it's rather like Boccaccio's short story about the innocent girl who went out into the desert in search of religious truth and only managed to have the devil put back into her virgin hell. We could pass the time like that. I mean *The Decameron's* structure is really an almost natural way of combining grim reality with the art of story-telling. There is the plague outside and the storytellers inside. When Chaucer adapted that form to his own specific needs in the *Canterbury Tales* he really was taking over a genre which unlike the novel is most suited to the oral tradition here in Africa. There is the same irreverent zestful treatment of values, institution and beliefs; the same go-getting specificness say in the "Wife of Bath's Prologue" and putting the devil back into hell. You have the fabric and texture of life being scrutinized under a microscope with a no-holds-barred attempt to put people's happiness first before anything else. The ridicule and absurdity which society weaves into our lives is exactly magnified, as is the phoneyness of literary and art-with-a-capital-A attitudes. The Spanish picaresque novel has the same robustness, the gnomic grit. This is the art that's most true to ordinary people lives.

'Of course, the notion of "ordinary people" is an artificial one, as is that of extraordinary people. *Don Quixote* probably appeals to everybody, the sort of everybody who is supposed to be in all of us. It's merely the way people translate the pleasure they get from a reading which sets up the differences between serious and popular literature. The sort of "my pleasure is aesthetic and refined" and "my pleasure is down to earth" kind of difference. I think one simply ought to write as though one would be understood by everyone. You know the way a "classic" that has become general reading is always explained away by things like "it appeals to the everyman in all of us"; this everyman is an artificial creation made to encompass the general notions of man which the church and our philosophers preach. The morality play *Everyman* is not at all different from any proselytizing sermon say by a Salvation Army corporal or by a dustman who has suddenly seen the light. Or by Lord Brethren Himself. The notion of a grand staircase of choices leading up to the grave or of kings climbing up and down from dust to throne to dust or of Romeo stepping in and out of ecstasy is as well trodden as the path from birth to death. The pleasure we get from observing these antics is made up of several layers from which each one of us is free to choose whatever suits us best. It's another matter if you have to write an essay on it, or a review or just a timid notice of the event. In half the time, we joust with windmills whenever we think we know why we enjoy one book and not another.

'Since reading is an industry in its own right somebody somewhere is getting the profits. Publishers, critics, lecturers, second-hand booksellers and shoplifters. It's a complete study of how parasites and their hosts exist. At the same time there are all the rest of them breathing down the writer's neck telling him he must write in a certain way and not in another way; and there are those who think that because they have read what has been written have got a perfect right to say just about anything to the writer and he is supposed to take it calmly. Every man is a walking collection of aphorisms. The thing about a story lurking round every corner, and a novel resting uneasily inside every human skull. Nonsense. Apart from the initial spark of creativity in the best and worst parts of the first book, the writer's road is littered with crumpled contracts, bleeding symbols, and broken teeth, all in the wake of big business. The hidden persuaders are well dug in behind the ramparts and they know exactly how to stimulate that kind of phoneyness which a complacent reading public takes for its own good taste. At the same time you get the heels crunching down on your spine to make you think that objectivity is possible where such things as language rule. Roland Barthes has tried to blow up that balloon and quite successfully too, though they have, of course, an in-built eject-mechanism and he will probably find himself falling into oblivion without a parachute.'

Liz, who was staring out through the window, said non-committally:

'Those paratroops are still coming down. Something big is going on over there.'

Cicero sighed:

'Why can't they settle their disputes with a couple of football games? It would be less costly in lives and money and buildings and brain damage. But no, it has to be war. That's where all this science gets you. Each side's scientists have to prove they are as up-to-date and as brilliant as the other side. And so they continue to invent these infernal nuclear and neutron bombs. It happens in writing too. You've got to beat all the others in your field if you're ever going to make any mark. It's the same in all the other kinds of research. Knowledge has become a most devastating kind of game. In this room, suppose, we are a microcosm of that kind of mug's game. The Faculty of Arts! I hate competition. It's so soul-destroying and seems so necessary. But I don't get any kind of kick from the survival-of-the-fittest syndrome. I think it's sick. Life has been possible on earth for a thousand million years from minute masses of protoplasm which increased their structure's complexity to become the fauna and flora of today, some of which is stewing with ennui in this room. The weakest goes to the wall. The meek are no longer blessed. The persecuted, the peace-makers, the pure, the merciful, the seekers after righteousness, the mourners, and the poor, are all damned. According to the gospel of natural selection they cannot survive the struggle for existence. Man, if that's what reality is, then I'm all right, Jack, locked up inside my own head.

'It is the ruin and not the original which moves men; our

Zimbabwe Ruins must have looked really shit and hideous when they were brand-new. But now their ruin imposes itself upon the grand imagination of even thousands who have never actually seen them. The *ubi sunt* emotion. The melancholy of the *peregrinus*. We are wanderers, I suppose, of the refugee kind, being the ruin, not the original of ourselves.'

Liz laughed. She said:

'It's the postcard effect. Transfer any face on to paper in charcoal or colour and at once something in it will strike you as not having been there before. It's not the same as the camera effect. But it's the kind of thing some people think of as poetry. Things like:

> The room seemed empty
> Like my soul
> I had no way
> To find you
> Anywhere
> My heart was cold.'

Otolith asked:

'Who wrote that?'

'I've just made it up,' Liz said scratching her vividly transparent head. 'It's not difficult to make things up like that. The difficulty is really knowing what is and what is not poetry. Is this poetry:

> The day before I left
> I felt so sad
> Life beheld me from afar
>
> The sun is set
> The raven flown
> The dark sad truth is in your eyes?'

'I don't care if it is not, but I like it very much,' Cicero said. 'It has within it that which touches upon where my thoughts and feelings come from and where they go. Surely you did not make that up right now.'

She said:

'Not exactly. I wrote them years ago before this war and have just committed them to memory because I thought I had forgotten them. You see, I had written them about a very good friend of mine and when things went wrong between us I burnt everything there was to remind me of him. But, as I said, I must have—it does not matter. I was at London University and lived in a squat close to Euston Station, reading literature and

92

painting and drawing and writing poems and drinking bad wine. It was fun. I would write in my diary things like "Who the hell fucked me last night?" It was sad too, for there were as usual lots of nice young people who had no money and no roof, who were ageing fast while still thinking of what the future held for them. But it was a good and warm time as when "the winter is past, the rain is over and gone; the flowers appear on the earth; the time of the singing of birds is come; and the voice of the turtle is heard in our land.".'

Cicero, pleased, muttered the praises of Solomon. He said, as if to himself:

'And even now that you're so far away, I'm learning fast, I'm learning every day that quiet patience that you left to me, exchanging it for all I had to say.'

He was probably referring to one or other of his parents.

'Do recite some more of your poems. They make you seem more human.'

She laughed.

'You mean, more ridiculous,' she said. 'All right.'

There was an untranslatable gleam in her eyes.

> 'It's good to smile
> And speak English
> After a while
> Of speaking a language
> I don't like very much
>
> It made a change
> To meet someone
> With a name
> I'd never heard before.'

'Is that a poem?' Cicero asked.

But she said: 'Is this one—

> The ways of the world are devious
> But the paths of the soul divine
> Some have the power to bring into essence
> All that is there in the mind?'

'The first one makes me smile all the way to my room,' he said. 'But the second one makes me think in a headache sort of way and thinking can easily turn to contempt, but it illuminates from the inside of the skull. It's part of everything we can do. Why does poetry seem such an intensely and peculiarly human activity?'

'Ah, seems!' Otolith exclaimed, delighted. 'Claudius, who

unseated the Dane, was good at seeming and smiling. The balls in a juggler's hands seem never to touch the hand and most art is like that.'

And from behind me, in the dressing gown, a voice said:

'Walk away from your shadow and you will draw gasps of wonder. You know the way nature sculpts driftwood by decay and corrosion, and sculpture in such a way as to make paltry the efforts of our finest sculptors. It's like what he said about ruins. And especially in ancient carvings that have become mutilated by time, you find the same power that impresses us. Old Latin and Greek sculptures seem more beautiful to us precisely because of their time-eaten and mutilated look. Our obsession with antiques, too. And old architecture? Relics. As though some taboo was broken long ago and the fascination of that Faust-like craftsmanship still fills our minds with a possible immortality. The fashioning out of unities from dissonant, disparate and disfigured experiences is at the heart of art. Blake touched on the power that drives us so. His tiger burned brightly with it. Yeats too sought to translate that transcendent madness into the ordinary instances of our lives. It's like the way cancerous growths slowly but surely gnaw away at the under-surface of our thoughts and feelings. That enigmatic smile of the Mona Lisa is probably the best outward expression of the rank and terminal cancer deep inside her and her age. It's as though some secret fungi, some impossible bacillus infects us through an incision in our mind and imagination with a fatal yearning for beauty, terror, horror, creativity. Certainly the common imagination portrays artists as consumptive, tubercular and generally sickly. Thomas Mann's works seem exclusively to consider this worth exploring, not just in artists but also in musicians and other upper-caste progenitors of the sublime. The twentieth century has made us quite aware of the horrors we are capable of perpetrating against each other and therefore we can look dispassionately at Bosch's paintings without unnecessarily consigning them to the limited shelf labelled Medieval Terrors.

'Some psychiatrists today diagnose disenchantment with social structures as a disease and proceed to inflict a cure on the patient. Some of our greatest writing comes from writers in a state of mind of disillusion, disenchantment and dismay. The films on television and in the cinemas, those that have the uttermost sex and violence, seem to instil into certain sectors of society dread, fear and the suspicion that the sex and the violence can be directly transferred from the celluloid image into the corrupt and murderously depraved intention of an actual criminal act. Censorship results from an irrational fear of contamination; if it was rational then time would be well spent censoring all those actual instances of history where grim brutality has wrestled with grim brutality. The bombing of Dresden. The experience of the concentration camps. Hiroshima. Tasmania. All those instances when societies have imposed upon each other with rape and violence and disenchantment. George Orwell's Big Brother, by actually erasing and rewriting history, was doing this censorship very rationally. But we have to live at the mercy of Mary Whitehouse and other moral philanthropists like her. Every play in England has to be morally censored. There was even a blasphemy trial once concerning a poem about a centurion contemplating the homosexual possibilities of Jesus Christ's body. This kind of thing is unthinkable, but it happens.

The Bible was my very first porn book. I remember being very excited by the passage in "Kings" where the girl Tamar is raped by her brother. I used to masturbate while reading that over and over. I suppose incest intrigues me. I was a good Christian but I just couldn't make out how we were all not related to each other because there was only Adam and Eve to start with. This for me was the inward secret of the Christians and it explained why they always looked as if they had just had a fantastic orgasm together. And then there were the really violent scenes when the kings would be assassinating and massacring each other. The one I like best, because it was so unbelievable, was the young man's speech to Jehu:

Thou shalt smite the house of Ahab thy master
That I may avenge the blood of my servants the prophets
And the blood of all the servants of the Lord at the hands
    of Jezebel.
For the whole house of Ahab shall perish:
I will cut off from Ahab him that pisseth against the wall
    and him that is shut up and left in Israel:
And the dogs shall eat Jezebel in the portion of Jezreel
    and there shall be none to bury her.

Ahab and his seventy sons are killed, as are all "his great men, and his kinsfolk, and his priests"; indeed Kings II 9 and 10 are just a great orgy of killing and I have always thought that Amin learnt this particular section of the whiteman's Bible rather well. But it was the manner of Jezebel's death which really impressed me and reinforced in my mind all the European History I had learnt. I've got a Bible. This is it: "And when Jehu was come to Jezreel, Jezebel heard of it; and she painted her face, and tired her head, and looked out at a window. And as Jeru entered at the gate, she said, Had Zimri peace, who slew his master? And he lifted up his face to the window, and said, Who is on my side? Who? And there looked out to him two or three eunuchs. And he said, Throw her down. So they threw her down: and some of her blood was sprinkled on the wall and on the horses: and he trode her under foot. And when he was come in, he did eat and drink, and said, Go, see now this cursed woman, and bury her: for she is a king's daughter. And they went to bury her: but they found no more than her skull, and the feet, and the palms of her hands. Wherefore they came again and told him. And he said, This is the word of the Lord saying, In the portion of Jezreel shall dogs eat the flesh of Jezebel: And the carcass of Jezebel shall be as dung upon the face of the field."

'I first read that when I was nine years old. From that time onwards I just couldn't stand dogs. I kept remembering "the palms of her hands" and I would look at my own palms and try to think out a world in which such things were religious. You see, all the whites that I saw kept dogs and every whiteman's dog is well-fed and looks as if it's always eaten better food than I and as if it's always lived in better houses, which is all true. Every whiteman and his dog was my enemy, my terror, my specific horror. And when there were strikes and riots, the policemen always brought Alsatians that were trained by being constantly starved and maddened by having black human meat waved in their faces from the other side of their cages. South Africa and Rhodesia were always full of whites with dogs. You could really see how a whiteman's dog was even more rabidly racist than the whiteman himself. I could see all this in the palms of my hands.

'And then I went to England and it was really bad there because all the white friends I made always made a comment about how my palms were paler than my hands and face. They never understood why I would simply explode whenever they did that, and it would be the last time I would speak to them. Finally, a psychology lecturer suggested that I see an analyst. I did. But I never quite knew how he'd cured me. He was black, but he wasn't Franz Fanon. My palms stopped radiating their

96

uncanny awareness of how canine the world was; but my mind was still digesting the idea though Jews were not exactly thrown to starved Alsatians but were gassed and cremated alike, it was still the same world thinking itself religious and pure in the Mendel manner. I started to read palmistry and began to read my palms and other people's palms. But whenever moral philanthropists begin to preach what should be read and seen and what should not be read and seen I think of their Bible which they impose on everybody and think of the masturbation and the palms of Jezebel's hands.

'In Africa, of course, it seems we have inherited the shit kind of Christian religiosity and have fast caught up with the developed world in hypocrisy and moral standards. Bible people have become our political leaders. Bible people have become our teachers and headmasters. Bible people sit on our city councils. Bible people are the prison warders, the hospital doctors, nurses and orderlies. Bible people have taken over from the colonial administrator, taken over the rigorous super-vision of of the African mind. Black moral philanthropists have taken over from the nineteenth-century Victorian philanthro-pists and they are pushing tracts underneath our door. You find them everywhere: in industry, in agriculture, in the bed-room and in the toilet. And they are all holding out the pale palms of their hands. That's why I am living here; living like this! And now they are dropping from the sky in thousands to fulfil my nightmare.'

The change in his face had been so gradual that until now I had not noticed it. His face had apparently tightened around itself to emphasize the cheekbones, the slightly prominent chin, the emaciated cheeks, and the unhealthy ashy skin. He looked much smaller than I had thought; certainly the dressing gown seemed several sizes too large for him. The fingers, which he drummed on the arm of the chair, were ingrained with dirt, and the nails were long and broken; the flesh between the thumb and the forefinger was patterned with grey and the knuckles looked as hard and as weather-corroded as bronze left for too long in the sun and wind.

Liz had her back to the window now. She said irritably:

'Do we have to talk about race all the time?'

Cicero pounced gently.

'You started it by talking about guns.'

She seemed to wake out of an inner delirium.

'Yes, the guns. Does anybody here know anything about guns?'

'As much as anyone out there,' Otolith said. 'Where are these guns you keep talking about?'

She indicated a large cardboard box in the corner behind the door. Otolith, after exclaiming 'Wow!' went to work. Liz put the palm of her hand on my shoulder. I did not have to ask her.

'Yes, it's serious,' she said, 'but it doesn't show much until the very last moment when it would be too late anyway. She is a brave girl. You take care of her for me. I know she will look after you well.'

She looked out at the window, her face gathering together a faraway and remote gaze. I followed the line of her look. Parachutes still fell from the sky and there were so many of them that for the first time I felt fear. This was certainly a big thing. Did it mean the end of my life in this house? We could hear the low and distance-muffled crack and roar of guns and shells. Now and then sudden explosions of smoke, dust and shrapnel, pinpointed where men were being ground into the special creation we call earth. Who was fighting whom? Would they come for us. I had for so long taken life as I found it that it was not before Liz spoke again that I realized that I was suddenly afraid. Afraid for Helen and for myself; but most afraid of once more having to admit deepest in myself that the absurdities going on out there held the power of life and death over Helen and me. And Liz, and Otolith, and Cicero and the man in the dressing gown. Yes, and Liz's boy who was still avidly reading the war comics I had given him.

'Does she mean so much to you?' Liz asked.

I nodded. For the first time in my life I knew I would give myself and give myself unreservedly not to an idea of humanity but to a girl called Helen.

And I remembered a letter from long ago from a friend I met on the road. She had been as penniless as I was and I had played the guitar in railway stations and in the underground to make some money to get by without being utterly destitute. It was not really a letter but I think an attempt on her part to recapture something of the freedom and poverty and openness of those days. She was small and always reminded me of a sunflower and her eyes were pale grey and she had bitter memories of a stepfather whose attentions had finally forced her to leave home without telling her mother what was going wrong. We lived together for a while on the bare floorboards of her squat in Highgate and, though I was still too defensive to notice, I was happy she was happy for both of us. It was not much of a life I was leading, mucking about in libraries every day to find newer and newer material, all that would keep my freelance articles flowing. I was then still naive enough to think that one ought to write only when one 'feels' like it inside; this meant that I could not finish many of the stories and articles I began. Anyway the guitar came in useful sometimes in a single day, raising as much as that day's food and drink for Barbara and me. She did beadwork and batiks and hoped one day to get a grant to study fashion design.

We would have been really happy if I had been more mature. I was childish about women then and foolish and jealous and given to sudden despairing dramatics which later I realized were merely an attempt on my part to act on her the writer's supposed impulsive nature. I was still insecure enough to want to freak people out. Anyway, it was not much of a life for her. She tried to tell me what it was that was going wrong but I was not listening to what she was saying but to the note of anger and hurt in her voice and I reacted to that by forcing a quarrel. It is very sordid when two people of our sort quarrel: if we'd been straight hippies it would have been all right. Our life style gave us no lifelines for such an emergency. It was all over in an instant. And then she wrote those lines I still recall clearly because when I read them I was on my way back to Africa. She was trying to describe the African image she had seen but at the same time she was making an incision into a time when she had been the other side of the Common Market.

The letter went on: 'When you look serene and calm it does not matter that you can't hold your cup; that your hand shakes too much. When you smile sardonically at all those who rushed to see the fight outside the bistro, it doesn't matter that the night is cold and raining and you don't want to go home. When the night is wet and cold and you've walked all over Paris and you feel so tired and old and you sit and watch the dawn break in a tiny café, you'll find it doesn't matter that you're shivering outside, that your eyes will not stay open, that the restaurant man tells you to get your blueboots off his clean chairs. And when you finally find that the cold old night is gone and you've eaten some elastic bread and watched the Paris dawn on a grey and rainy morning you've drunk some scalding tea that you couldn't really swallow and the man asks you to leave for he couldn't read the bill that you dropped in your hot chocolate. You walk off to the metro and you eat something that comes from the confectionary machine and you sleep and you smoke while you're waiting for the train until you had to go off to your waiting room . . . It really doesn't matter that you've had a lousy birthday, that your life goes on the same way, that there's still two whole months ahead, for in your heart you know you don't have to do a thing you don't want to in the long run anyway. There are people all around who care. You'll meet them every day.' And she signed her name on top of a cloverleaf: 'Barbara'.

And I remember wondering whether she was pregnant because I had read in Yukio Mishima that Japanese girls who want a child wear kimonos with cloverleaf designs. She had sprinkled it with a little mysterious perfume she had always worn but had not told me its name. My sunflower. Now here she was in another totally different being giving me another chance. I had matured somewhat. I had in those intervening years seen too much of how misery comes because we are totally meaningless to each other. Ignorance is to be filled with oneself. But I who had been ignorant of my fellow human beings for such a painfully long time had looked out through the incision from where I was closely packed within myself. I would make no demands anymore. Gratitude would not turn into guilt and friendship would not turn into contempt. Never would I take the easiest way by a lie. And so the thing I had thought I took for granted sat there, destitute, like me, and we stayed by the empty cup and talked again of things to come and of moments past until the waiter threw me out. And you went off to the Metro for money so we could drink that night and I glided all the way to my room. Happiness can turn to pain, she said, I often wondered what went wrong and hope that you'd forgive me if you knew the things I did in my sorrow. And she turned her face towards Birmingham. But I still gaze at that sunflower and think with her images about how a heart of gold turned into stone.

Those paratroopers; their growing menace. We couldn't have much time left, whatever it was that was coming; for I am not a pacifist. A rifle in my hands would be life taking me as suits me. Helen at my side would be the first time I had found the thread of life between what is inside me and the devastation out there. We were six; seven, counting the boy. I nodded again.

Liz had looked away again out at the window.

'If there's any trouble,' she said, 'with those paratroopers or any others, remember that Helen is a deadly shot. She will want to do her share of the fighting. And you mustn't try and stop her. She knows what she will be doing.

She answered before I asked the question:

'She fininished her training last month. And then the sickness was discovered and they forced her to leave her unit.'

'What was her unit?'

Liz said carefully:

'Will that make any difference?'

A long moment later she shook me by the shoulder and with a hint of mockery in her voice repeated her question:

'Will it make any difference?'

I held her gaze easily:

'No,' I said feeling sure now.

'She will tell you herself if she wants to. In fact I think she will tell you tonight. I have never known her to beat about the bush. She is young, remember that, but she learns very fast. The only thing she is incapable of is learning to read and write. Some form of dyslexia. She is a very resourceful and forthright person. Satisfied?'

'I love her,' I said simply, feeling like a fool because Liz was smiling.

'Fine.'

She indicated the already-filled bookshelf:

'You can borrow any of those. They are all my favourites,' she said.

I selected a volume of Montaigne's *Essais*. She nodded, yawned:

'That ought to see you through to the next century,' she said.

'In the meantime I've got to start learning how to use one of those guns.'

Otolith, grim, handed me a machine pistol and ammunition.

'This can be useful too,' he said giving me a .38 service revolver.

Helen would teach me how to use both.

She was on the floor, bent over her drawings, when I came. She looked up, biting her lip, and nodded.

'Okay?'

I dropped down beside her, feeling awkward and self-conscious. The room was still the same but a subtle change had come over everything in it. Having always derided sentimentality and kept tenderness at bay by a rigorous and half-digested cynicism, I could not think of anything to say. And the guns in my hands made it all ridiculously unreal.

I threw the books on to the large armchair and indicated the guns:

'You'll have to teach me about these, Helen.'

But I was staring at the drawings.

'You know about changelings?' she said. 'I feel them all the time as though we were all changelings and not exactly what we appear to be—what I've been trying to draw all these days. There's so much missing inside where things ought not to be missing as though something indefinable was taken out of us long ago. Don't you feel that sometimes?'

I could have said I felt like that all the time. I could have said that's how everything seems to be most of the time. The ghastly emptiness that was always there when I awoke and when I was dreaming. The feeling of having died and yet not really died, of how one had been subtracted from all that makes life a living experience. I could have said it was the fear inside me of a world whose changes would never include a change for the better. Like hearing in the dead of midnight some phantom figure moving about hammering nails into all the things one had learnt to take for granted. Like walking down a street feeling uniquely aware of how it will always be like this, in spite of the warmth of bliss in the shining down of the sun and the feeling of how cold a comfort it was being there. I could have said again and again that I was discovering once more how infinitely a human condition despair was and not joy or love or just being there together. Hammering nails into a coffin in which the image of a whole historical notion lay with its arms crossed over its breast. Hammering nails into the palm of Jezebel's hand. And the blood streaming in the firmament, with not a single drop to save Faustus from the hour at hand.

All this which was happenning out there in the grim outside of our thoughts and emotions was finally approaching nearer and nearer to the unrefusing mortality of our block. I could no more have convinced myself that it was nothing to do with us than have hypnotized myself into believing that every ache out there was my ache and every bayonet flashing in the sun my bayonet. I could have thrown up my hands in disbelief and washed my hands and parried all with Pilate's question: What is truth? I could have said, It's these incredible situations which this impossible creation makes possible. But all this had nothing to do with the small lightning that flashed suddenly from the touch of her hand on my index finger; and there was the thunder incredibly uncoiling and uncoiling down to the last tendril in the innermost cellular world. Matthew Arnold's still sad music seemed to have ceased utterly, leaving us the sole inheritors of a silence-divining wasteland. Here was no pilgrim's progress, no mythical Sysiphus bound forever to push his rock, no Prometheus hurling defiance at Zeus even as he watches the vultures gorge themselves on his chained body. There was only Helen and me in a dusty room in a crumbling old and devastated building.

I had never killed before, but suddenly killing seemed only a small irrelevancy to the interior happenings taking place in the house. That they were indissolubly connected to what was happening out there I could not deny, but the connection was as ephemeral and irrelevant as the issues of killing and dying. We had, I suppose, talked ourselves into a mood whose shadow had outgrown us. That was the fate of any thinking being. No longer could we register the temperature of the blood in us, the reading of the instincts and archetypal triggers; we had so given ourselves up for lost that there was no meaning in such things, only a meaninglessness which cybernetics could trace on a graph. At the same time the thoughts that controlled our feelings were not those of where straight lines come from nor where they go. There is no centre either, nor circumference, but as it were spiralling nebulae, galaxies beyond galaxies, exploding wildly outward, hurtling away towards the incredible infinite that lay beyond the boundaries in which we had lingered.

It was raining that day I first returned to the Faculty. The bombers had gone and I crawled out from underneath the mass of concrete and girders which had miraculously stopped short of killing me. I could see no one else in the whole length of the gap-toothed street. Dust and blood and sweat had caked my body and it was uncomfortabie in my dirty jeans. I got my bearings again and found the place where I had hidden my rucksack. As I hitched the wretchedly heavy thing on to my back, the smoke and flames crackling out from the gaping windows and doorways on either side of the street showered the áir with an indefinable and stark horror. There was something uncommonly surreal about it all; war in my mind had been something one read in comics, a news-flash on a television screen, a photo-album of photogenic victims fleeing in terror from the dramatic burst of napalm. But here it was, right there in that part of Africa where I had been born into the world; right there where I had dreamed and learned of new things, and argued the whole night through about literature and the fate of my country; right there where the bishop and the priest and Smith had intrigued and finally come to blows; right there where hope had been pinned like a medal on the Patriotic Front and its guerillas; right there between black Africa and white Africa. And I had come home from Oxford and London where I had learnt nothing and forgotten nothing. It was raining, a light drizzling rain, that looked and felt more like an attitude than an actual occurrence called weather.

I uncorked the flask of whisky I had brought and wandered up the street towards the building which Owen had indicated. Owen was then living in the room where soon I would live; he had already painted the mural on the wall, saying of it: 'I've decided to call it War.' But all there was on the wall was the black woman, the blood-red giant cat, the black archer, the falcon, the zebra, and the thick growth of jungle. It reminded me of Rousseau and a primitive painting of a naked black man vainly fleeing from a pouncing leopard. The stylized nature of the mural made it a kind of emblematic necessity. The whisky was still burning my throat when I crossed a derelict playground and went round to the front of the building. I walked up to the top floor and listened to Owen releasing the three locks and unbolting the seven chains. As I stepped into the light to shake Owen's hand warmly, I did not know that soon he would go out there in a hysterical rage against 'everything' and be shot down by some unknown soldier.

Owen had been one of those brilliant students whom our country nourishes solely in order to break their spirit on the anvil of crude racial antagonism. He and I enjoyed the common and sordid freedom of being born in the slums and hacking our way out of them by the skin of scholarships. It gave both of us that inner knowledge of gritty insecurity which cements in some a love of intellectual pleasure and a particular distaste for the strictures of mediocre occupations. But whereas I fled the country, he remained and fought for the survival of his sanity among those whom he knew he could neither love nor trust.

Seeing him again, a hardy sapling among the varied soil of his books and notes, I could not guess how much the acids of the bitter and inconsolable experience of losing his nation had corrosively affected what inner reserves he had against despair. We had used to joke about being fucked out by everything but never to the extent of seeing the uttermost truth at the centre of the jest. There was the gulf—as we saw it—between student thinking and activities and the workers—themselves whom I did not feel we had any qualifications to lead in anything. I had seen how 'education' had given us too early the veneer of experience which our own elders mistook for mature and solid knowledge of a world that had rapidly ceased to be ours and had become a whiteman's playground for investment, good living, and casual tormenting of Caliban.

At the same time as I grew up, I ceased to see grown-ups as anything other than as perplexed as we were; the only difference was that they were burdened down by the ageing of the flesh and could think of death without any imaginative colouring to save them from the dark beating of its wings. The sense of having lost our nation was indivisible from the feeling of the nation having lost us; the smack of some incompetent fate made our eyes sting. Indeed, had there ever been a nation at all? The white pioneers and adventurers who had carved out for themselves farms and estates and had for a time exercised the pirate's right to booty were the sort of origins we had as one nation. That tribal adhesions had unstuck themselves from that experiment and, only united, we cast off the yoke that had left us with the responsibility of continuing the experiment under another brand name. At the same time the schools and colleges had churned out people like Owen and myself who had not the ruthless stamina required to breathe the mighty breath of a united nation. Was this not an expansion of the limits of the imagination rather than a down-to-earth nation planning exercise? Certainly, sympathies, ideas, dreams had suddenly been given limitless scope in excess of the actual and practical problem. Certainly, human means and ends had suddenly become inconsequential in the grand sacrifice. Certainly, human life, degraded to the level of nothing more than an inconvenience in the inevitable march through the corridors of historical transitions, was now the plaything for various beliefs, propositions, slogans, even a certain type of literature. Certainly, the way forward increasingly meant the progress of inhumanity rather than the extension of the very freedoms which had given it life. Certainly, the machine of the nation-state gave the citizen a prefabricated identity and consciousness made up of the rouge and lipstick of the struggle and the revolution.

Had we lost the African image or had the African image lost

us? Did it exist? Certainly, it had become an obscene idol, an altar of lost dreams, lost hopes, lost faith, lost silences; lives lost. It did not teach us the simple preciousness of all life; and by that standard could be judged no precious loss. But with an over-running flood it will make an utter end of the place thereof, and darkness shall pursue its enemies. Woe to the bloody city! It is full of lies and robbery; the prey departeth not; the noise of a whip, and the noise of the rattling of the wheels, and of the prancing horses, and of the jumping chariots. Our shadows had grown hideous and their sudden strength had sucked the heat out of our hearts. We were at once supremely ourselves and the caricature of them. The mind reeled between the mirage of a snug mud-hut in the middle of nowhere and the noise of a gong in a draughty city apartment. The chink of coins in a calloused palm—that palm of Jezebel which the dogs did not eat—and the noise of a rattle shaken in the night both soothed the prodigal as he beat his path homeward bound, teeth clenched tightly over caged bottom lip. A bloodless sunset hung like a curtain over the city. And when we lifted a corner of it, we saw our ourselves in the careless abandon of *assimillados* who have not forgotten their place.

From beyond the rim of the unknown, rose the preternatural urge to consume to the hilt the beads and art trophies in the whiteman's bin. We looked into the mirror, seeing only the disgust on a whiteman's face; we looked into the mirror, miming only the black-is-beautiful in a negro poet's imagination; we looked into the mirror teaching our children the use of skin-lightening creams and psychoanalysts. There was no place like home, only in the no-man's land where the water finds its own level; where there is no sense of gravity but that emanating from your neighbour's backyard; where there was no reality but the reality of minds perpetually dredged out of their own mud. The president of the United States accused Cuba of doing nothing. Vincennes was put out into the cold. Maoris at Waitemata Harbour were arrested in a show of strength. And another round of settlement talks ended with mutual disgust and recrimination. Harare boiled, making cabbage soup and Molotov Cocktails. Ian Smith wiped caviar from his penis and smothered newsmen with quotations from Kipling. 'There is no African problem,' agreed the Bishop. Meanwhile, a sociologist in a wrecked lift in the Sun Hotel shouted in a matter-of-fact gibberish 'Nothing left except the clothes they are wearing!'

And indeed, as I looked at Owen, I agreed that there was nothing of us left except the clothes we were wearing; nothing left except the paintings we painted on to the painted walls; nothing left except the poem and stories I sweated blood to bleed out of me; nothing left except the self-consciousness that could only give, and give unreservedly, in novels like this.

It is a short walk to the grave, only a drop of blood away; only a rational thought away; only a strong feeling away. There you meet all the versions of yourself that did not come out of the womb with you. It is of them that I write. But they have the face of all the ones who did come out with me; the ones who did no wrong but found themselves in the dock on trial for their innocence and their country; the ones who wear their skeletons on the outside, always in fear of massacres devastating the territory enclosed in their skull and feeling; the ones who have been exposed all their waking and dreaming life to the ordinance map of their own madness. In the street, it is always a car backfiring. Here, it is the sudden silence that startles me. There, it is the ageing flesh and waning mind, totally at the mercy of children who have grown old too. Beyond the edge of all that's conceivable there lies a hideous thing that would teach us to unwrap the bandage of cynicism from our wounds and reveal the eyes so long—too, too long—bound by it. But there is nothing to be seen but a city ruined, a mind diseased, and paratroopers suddenly dropping in thousands out of the unmoving sky.

Helen busily teaches me the parts and uses of the guns. Owen is dead. The changelings that occupy the time of her imagination are there stark and obscene in her drawings; their sharp red eyes glint with a poison redder than nerves. Are they that long-lost part of us which always turns up like a bad penny?

Strangely they remind me of my first love, a totally ill-advised affair with Owen's sister in the dragon crowds of football-crazed Harare. She made me feel caged in by the soft bars of her heart; she made me feel rooted in the middle of a universe that was totally composed of her eyes and lips and body, and every whim of the wind blowing into my face was an utterly sensuous experience; it seemed I was the dry land and she the sea, big and round around it. Strange ecstasies writhed in my mind; vivid and tortuous delights spun around the sun—a rainy sheen that threw its other-world hues on everything in my surroundings. At that time, she was still waiting to be discovered as the number one black actress to come out of Africa, a sort of noble savage version of Brigitte Bardot. The films and the stage were her one obsession; nothing else existed for her—as far as I know, nothing else does still. In the grimy whitewash and rabid concrete of Harare, the cinema held out for us the vision of another world in which adventure, passion, suspense, death, and rigorous painstaking dreaming still had a place and she decided it was her place. Nothing would stop her, not even the sombre recollection that black actresses never seemed to have anything other than playing the true Dostoevskian slave and drudge roles of servant and backdrop.

Owen and I liked photography and as soon as he could he bought a film camera and a projector. Tsitsi, his sister, was our star. I wrote the scripts and Owen was cameraman, producer and director. As we literally had no money worth sneezing about, we filmed only when and what was strictly necessary. Our films, conceived as intense poetic manias about African-ness, were for me exhilarating experiments in the use of illusion and reality to make statements about life with a capital L. Tsitsi was good; there is no other word for it. Put her into an empty room and at once it springs to life. She had that exotic and magical touch which made everything at her fingertips glow and radiate with life. And she could use every single nerve and muscle of her body to weave quixotic meanings, poignancies, painful dilemmas, into the most ordinary and mundane situation. Each time I saw her, talked to her, listened to her, it was as if she was a phantom and creation of my imagination rather than a person in herself. Had I known it then I would have said I was experiencing for the first time what it is to feel one's own brain and feelings beating in another person. And yet it was not like that at all. It was our youth gazing and explaining itself to us in adult and centuries-old terms. She was the insider.

What bound us together, Owen, Tsitsi, and I, seemed deeper, higher, and as round as all the sky. Dark moods glittering a little with shock at the wonder and grit of living alternated in our films with bitter hard-edged pictures of the racial turmoil around us. The fetid raucous afternoons of siesta in the shanty-towns, the sleek hastily erected streets with their façades of Woolworth merchandise and Burton tailoring, the rusty grating sound of distant railyards and Dickensian factories, and the shrill and piercing cries of a harmless madman strutting back and forth in Cecil Square—they were all like slides assembled to illustrate to Martian visitors what human life was like in my country. Looked at through the compound eye of the god-insect with its mosaic vision, the whole looked like some astounding impossibility.

But there I was, in my fraction and chink of light, oblivious of the unusual eye watching me, as I tore at my hairs because a critic had, in passing, written this about my short stories: 'It is clear that the writer does not have a high opinion of the black man. He is pompous and a bore, trying to fight liberation from western capitals while all the time wishing he was white. But the black man cannot really hide his identity, however hard he tries. By admiring the whiteman so much he is also accepting the whiteman's image of him.' And there was Owen, glaciated in his own separate pool of light, but gleaming with sympathy as he read: 'These stories are damaging to the morale of the world bent on liberation. In their present form they are even more damaging to the young writer. He should be given the chance to represent these stories on a more rational plane. Furthermore, they should be experiences which can be shared by people who want to know what it means to be in Southern Africa today.' When Tsitsi read this she sent me a long letter of scant praise and abundant despair and, after signing her name, added: 'PS—This is the final straw. I am instituting divorce proceedings. PPS—The children are as well as the cats and will fight for custody.' What a time she must have been through! Even her handwriting had suddenly changed from its customary upright roundness to a small inscrutable hysterical worm that would not remain horizontal. At first I thought it was a joke, a forgery and sent a telegram to enquire; the reply came soon enough: 'Devastated enough shame stop proceeding divorce love Tsitsi.' I referred the matter to Owen who said, yes, she was quite serious; had been unhappy for a long time. That decided it. After I had seen him off at Heathrow I roamed around London smoking incessantly, unable to settle down in any particular pub. I remember I was thrown out of the Charles Dickens when I insulted a barmaid and refused to apologize to her or to the manager to mollify her. As I landed on my bottom in the gutter I was muttering in clenched terms about racists and fascists. I dusted myself up and stalked down to El Vino's where I managed to sog myself into a permanent state of shock.

Though I had long foreseen my mistake in marrying—I am one of those who are incapable of putting up with anyone for longer than necessary—I had not really imagined that things would come to such a pass. She had to a certain extent always frightened me. Love exposes one to all kinds of hurts and misuse by the adored subject and I resented and feared this. Also, because I take sexual intercourse in its full demoniac sense of possession and impregnation, I could never accept that I was—yes, I was—doing this to one whom I felt so much for. That's how young I was, and still am, where women are concerned. I wanted not a wife but both a friend and a lover. At the same time, I knew that I was secretly hiding from myself my glee at being free. The misfortune was also an excuse to get frightfully drunk before I returned to the desk.

The impiety of a Puck is the sort of mood I get into whenever I feel injured by reviewers and the family; it is a sordid but exhilarating attempt to recapture the childish openness of my youth. Though this was dangerous in a London full of policemen and National Fronts who added spice to the victuals. The drink was steadily transforming me, it injected into me a belligerent impishness which I thought I had lost with the departure of my student days. It took the form of rapid and delirious recapitulations of my whole life, bits and pieces of which would suddenly flit into my mind like bars of half-remembered music. It was once audible, visible, tactile, fragrant and elusively bitter-sweet as it swept again and again through the plastic atoms of my mind. The very act of re-capitulation was itself enough; the finely-cut diamonds of specific memories were a bonus. I could have danced—all the million versions of me—danced on the point of a pin, so light and inexplicably subtracted I felt. It was, as Petronius said, that the soul craves what it has lost and wholly throws itself into the past.

Each memory is ringed round with its own particular emotion; a rich Burgundy glows around the pleasing incident; a pale almost transparent green colours the ones which hurt; the deep clarity of sky-blue dapples the emotion-charged encounters with the adult world; a hot and blinding orange simmers in the things I hated most. But all the times I was painting or writing or feeling, watched by a part of me that was then missing are suspended in the lucid transparency of a drop of distilled water incised at an angle by the setting sun. The sound of them was elastic like honey; it trickled into the inner ear as though gently nudged by the lingering pulses of distant drums. The pitch was none too clear, involving all of me in an embrace that was silently shrill as if the silver wires of cicadas' fluting were coiling round and round my mind. And there hung over it all like a pang and cruciation the hint of an impossible perfume. And like an inspiration it flashed through my deepest senses that, yes, it was exactly this which I felt about the women if I felt anything about. All the music and colour and tastes and scent that was like a lapis lazuli eagle tearing its beak at my vitals was the shock and essence of all that I felt about Tsitsi. And not really about her, because it was subtle, inward-directed; as though love was to read in another's face and eyes the complex evidence and evolution of oneself. Anything cracked will break at a touch and so to touch myself in another sense makes me afraid. And she is touching herself in me too—how can a man reveal it! That is how I lost Tsitsi, even in the first days. That is how I lost Barbara and is how man and woman will always lose each other. And so I sat there numbed by the drink and the sullen arrogance of my gloomy face. There was Puck; where was the Fool to chorus Lear through lightning and rain? For it was raining as I abruptly left El Vino's bent on seeking out a disco in the West End. No wonder I had always felt there was something infinitely incestuous about my feelings for her.

I flagged down a taxi. The yellows, reds, blues, and green of the streets streaming past the wet and magnifying windows, were, as they flicked past, faster and faster, rigidly withholding any secret memories they had ever had. I was a mere ribbon of trivial human information being passed through their machine intestines. They excreted me dead and relieved right at the door, where, as I paid and pocketed the change, and walked down the carpeted stairs towards the inhuman din or rock reggae punk and slurp-wet music, I was thinking sourly that small drops of water and words hollow out of a stone. There were hundreds of people on the maxi-size floor and at the tables, dancing, drinking, eating, all of them, as it were, out to exorcize their countless cares. I got a drink and sauntered to the edge of the floor. I do not like pop music; I dance to it, and I did, that night, like the artist as a young man yielding to an efficient science. I have always danced like one who wants no more that he is and prefers nothing else; it is the only way I know to unlock the rhythm of any unusual fate. Tsitsi's face was lambent in my whole imagination; I was saying goodbye. In a minute I could not stand waiting there on her doorstep in the rain. I walked away into a new and thumpy song. Her image had utterly disappeared from my mind. Even now as I write I cannot remember her face's features but only what they once made me feel. The coloured lights—once again, reds, blues, greens and the harsh not unacceptable music of the incredible heavy disco—made all the multitudes around me look like ghosts that flit after death or visions that delude the slumbering wit. I could have laughed then, or cried, for how could I presume to dissect the nature of things to find out what demands? Soon, Bob Marley was hoarsely singing the coming of Jah and more people poured on to the already packed-to-frenzy floor. I refilled my glass and settled down to the serious science of unwinding, dancing with a girl who appeared from nowhere smiling secretly like an honest temptation and she danced so well I could not take my eyes off her. When the song ended we fought our way to the bar and sat back in our seats to talk about nothing but the heat of the moment. Though I woke up in her bed next morning in Earl's Court I remembered nothing except that she was American and was very demanding and it was easy to get on with her.

Far off in Beverley Hills, where Tsitsi lives now with her cats and memories, she is like a siren imprisoned in a vast aquarium howling a thin and honeyed melody which the faces ranged round it cannot hear though they see the tiny bubbles of its anguish streaming to the surface. I could never admit her youth and blindness until it was too late and we could only meet at the table across the gaze of our two children who could only make me think sadly that now I had two other versions of her as well. I had not seen much of them; Tsitsi did not want me to 'mess them up like you've messed yourself up' and besides I had not tried to contest her exclusive rights over them. I was and had always been a bad bachelor. We had not been together much. When she came over to England, she was engrossed in her film and I was heading for my breakdown in Oxford and enjoying it. Finally, she wanted a divorce willingly and assented to it. It was a mistake to have married the African Dream. I do not think it was any kind of dream to her, but a nightmare of neuroses which she finally could do without. It was not only unreal but not even a shadow of any substance other than the —for her, empty—talk of seminars and tutorials about the versions of human beings that exist in books. Though her film work brought her into intimate association with the creation of illusory reality, she nevertheless had a powerful and human awareness of—as she said—'the importance of being one's self.' And she was earnest; especially when Owen and I would jump into deep waters about it and reduce the house into one hell of a sounding board about what the Cretan meant when the Cretan said all Cretans are liars.

But I suddenly changed and she suddenly changed and the marriage changed us inside-out for the worse. I could not live on dreams, but scholarships, in my waking state. And I think in marrying her I was trying to marry a part of Owen, and not anything about her. Besides, I had no money and what destroyed the heart out of the marriage was that, as soon as I found out that money could not be comfortably scorned without wrecking Tsitsi's life, I simply gave up and she could not forgive that.

I am haunted by a thousand things I ought to have been and done; but the fiercest of them is that about making money. Orwell's Gordon Comstock went through the whiteman's version of it. I could never accept that making money is a virtue in itself or even in its provision of food for the loved one. It therefore became an evil necessity, like moving the bowels behind a bush when the bus stops. But there are those who write their best poems only when sitting and heaving on a toilet seat, at once giving birth to shit and to poetry, those inseparable twins. I cannot do that. I can only write when I have slept well, eaten well, drunk well, and am feeling well. But I can also write when all these conditions are not satisfied. I discovered this by accident when I was starving in Highgate and Barbara had left me to stew in my own juice. It seems to be a perpetual condition of my state that I should periodically attach and detach myself to the wandering humanity out there in the street, and call each attachment a profound and loving thing. It does not even have to happen by design; nowadays no single heart is safe from the passions of an accidental glance. Irony is not a strong enough breastplate against Cupid's arrows. There is nothing for it but to accept that Helen is all that I have always wanted.

A shell slammed into the derelict house opposite. There was a thud-clap report and a blinding flash. Another followed, and then another. As the unending salvo burst and exploded all around us, Helen threw herself to the floor and shouted:

'Get down!'

I was standing at the window, transfixed by what I was seeing. The walls shook, cracking in many places, and plaster dust fell. Then Helen twisted my leg from under me and I fell flat on my face. As I did so, half the room was torn out like wrapping paper: the spine-chilling room thundered dinningly at the core of all my senses, tearing out in a split-second chunk after chunk of deafening silence. I had too late jammed raw palms into my ears. As the bricks and burst water pipes showered down, I was, like a puppet, jerked backwards by the leg, scraping my face and elbows and chest on the bare floor. The bricks and pipes and ceiling beams smashed down where an instant before my body had lain; shattered and plunged through the sudden hole there. Screams rose from the workshop below; earth-cursing screams. I rolled with Helen on the floor till we lay directly underneath Owen's mural which still was untouched. But before we could take a first breath, another salvo scraped the roof from overhead, hurling it away like a paper-thin thing. It seemed the mind-wrenching bang had sucked the heat out of the sun, so cold was the horror. I clenched my lips against the rising hysteria. The rubble falling crashed down upon us but it was like feathers compared to that terrible explosion. I felt the sharp and human-hot breath escape from Helen's lips and when I looked down at her clinging convulsively tight to me where her face had been there was a red spurting wound. Bits of bone and flesh from her stuck on my chest and neck. Her eyeballs hung on threads of flesh: one of them was flung aside into her hair, and the other where her nose should have been. How white her teeth were in all that blood! It was as if she had bared them in the effort of that last breath which I distinctly heard. Her arms and legs still pressed tightly around me and as I gazed and gazed where her face should have been, the shells in quick succession crunched into the house which now shook like a living thing that is dying in agony. The first slammed my face into Helen's, the second and third brought down the mural in a bone-splintering mass. I could hear Cicero screaming over and over NO! NO! His voice—clamant in the sudden cessation of the bombing—howled with a choking soul-broken sound across the city: No! No! No! No!

The insane sanity of his cry shocked me back to my senses. With dawning horror, I slowly unstuck my face from hers. Dreamily, I brought up my uninjured hand and wiped my face and inspected the palm which had come away full of her blood dripping from my face. Before I could turn aside, I had begun to vomit epileptically on to her face and when I desperately wrenched my retching body from her the pain of the bricks and pipes and beams pinning me down upon her shot up my spine until I thought I would drown in vomit and pain. When finally I looked up, I saw coming towards the city centre, towards us, coming over the rabble flattened landscape, the thousands and thousands of face-blackened paratroopers.

There was dead silence, no shots fired at the advancing deadly insect-multitude. The very sky behind them was lit up with a transcendent flame.

As I looked at them, they seemed to cut a swathe through all that barred their way, and to glory in the ruin that marked their path.

I picked up the machine pistol that had fallen from Helen's arms and, even as the flies fought fiercely to glut their appetite on Helen's blood, I cradled the gun into position and waited for them to get into range.

Smash, Grab, Run

Let the minutes unleash
The bullets Brixton wishes
Barbed wire is the ivy on my walls
Acrid cordite like mist in autumn
Dissolves the harsh street into pellucid cameos
Think how the striking truncheon outpaces thought
How the burgeoning Molotov cancels discussion
And for just this once in my black British life
Exploded the atoms in me into atoms of power
Let each viewfinder's instant exorcize
The pictorial myths complacency devises
Each hurtling brick aimed to smash this
    enchanter's glass
Aimed to loot the truths for so long packaged in lies
I am the hundreds of putrid meat in English prisons
In derelict houses, in borstals, the millions of
    condemned meat
Who let the grim unleash their canned grime.

Oxford, Black Oxford

A few rusty spears of sunlight had pierced through the overhead drizzling clouds. Behind the gloom of rain and mist, I could see a wizened but fearfully blood-shot sun. And everywhere, the sweet clangour of bells pushed in clear tones what secret rites had evolved with this city. Narrow cobbled streets, ancient warren of diverse architecture all backed up into itself, with here there and everywhere the massive masonry of college after college. Sudden and thrifty avenues winding past close-packed little shops. And the Bodleian which American Margaret portrayed as an upside-down artichoke. The Cornmarket with its crowded pavements, its rebelliously glossy and supermarket look: did Zuleika Dobson ride past, her carriage horses striking up sparks from the flint of the road? Myth, illusion, reality were all consumed by the dull gold inwardness, narrowness, the sheer and brilliant impossibility of all as the raindrops splashed and the castanets of stray sunlight beams clapped against the slate roofs, walls and doorways—I walked slowly towards All Souls. My mind an essay to itself.

Drawing apart the curtains, opening the windows, to let in not the driving snow, but the hail of memories. The reek and ruin of heat and mud-huts through which a people of gnarled and knotty face could not even dream of education, good food, even dignity. Their lifetime was one long day of grim and degrading toil, unappeasable hunger whose child's eyes unflinchingly accused the adults of some gross betrayal. The foul smells of the pit latrines and the evil-sweet fumes of the ever-open beer halls, these infiltrated everything, from the smarter whitewashed hovels of the aspirant middle class to the wretched squalor of the tin and mud-huts that slimily coiled and uncoiled together like hideous worms in a bottomless hell. And here I was in Oxford thinking of the castanets of stray sunlight, calmly going to my tutorial in All Souls.

A sudden downpour made me run the last few yards into All Souls. The blood-shot mind up there was now completely shrouded by the heavy clouds coming in from the east. Stephen was already waiting outside the tutorial room. I was shaking and brushing the rain from my clothes. Stamping my feet on the faded mat. He smiled.

'Wretched weather,' he said.

'Stinking rain.'

'I hear you were sozzled last night. Had a brush with the porter.'

118

'As usual,' I said. 'But what brush up? I can't remember a thing.'

'Thought you wouldn't, actually.' He leaned back against the wall, hands in his pockets, ankle over ankle. 'He caught you climbing back in. He's got a black eye to show for it.'

Shit. I had forgotten to check my mail. There was probably a summons to the dean in it. Not again, for Chrissake. But I said in an off-hand way, 'Bloody uppity these porters, if you ask me. When a bloke is quietly sneaking back into his rooms, they make a fuss.'

'You weren't quietly sneaking back to your rooms. Apparently you were howling the Halellujah Chorus and cursing some unfortunate called Margaret.'

He blinked, asked, 'Is she *the* Margaret in St Hilda's? Rumour, you know, about you and her whatsit.'

'Can't say, old man. I haven't the foggiest about last night,' I said, too, ruefully. 'I managed to finish the bloody essay this morning. With a little help from Scotch. That funny malt we got at Smiley's.'

'Lethal concoction that.'

I could see he still wanted to drive home his point. He did.

'I heard it's not the dean this time. It's the walrus himself who wants to see you. I'm wondering what you're doing here actually.'

The Warden. Damn it.

'The damn walrus can bloody sing while waiting.'

'Language, dear boy. Language.'

The language of power.

'Sod it. And sod Old English too,' I said briskly. Changing the subject. 'Have you done yours?'

'Yes and no. It's still under unfinished business.'

The white-hot bitch. He had never produced a single essay for all the tutorials we had had together. Nobody seemed to care. Certainly he himself did not give a fig. I sighed.

'So I'll still have to read mine yet again.'

'You'll have to do the honours, I'm afraid.'

'Yeah, honky. Sure. Why not?'

'West Indian lingo, isn't it?'

'No, I'm just dying for a drink.'

He produced his hip flask, a silver and leather thing. We drank.

'Rather good, what?'

'Quite, O shit, quite.'

'Always wanted to ask where you learned your English, old

boy. Excellent. Even better than most of the natives in my own hedge. You know. Wales.'

'It's the national lingo in my country.'

'It is not bambazonka like Uganda?'

'Actually yes, your distant cousins are butchering the whole lot of us.'

'Mercenaries, eh. Sorry old man. Money. Nothing personal.'

Before I could say anything, he went on casually, 'Here he comes.'

Dr Martins-Botha, in jeans and anorak, was stamping his boots on the mat and shaking the rain from his person, from his umbrella.

'Sorry I'm late. The traffic. Come in, come in.'

The book-lined shelves. The desk in the corner at the end. With nothing on it but a glass paperweight. And the three chairs close to the single-bar electric fire which Dr Martins-Botha switched on as we sat down.—'Anywhere.'—and began to arrange ourselves and our papers.

'Brr,' he said. 'Brr,' he repeated. And SNEEZED.

As he blew his nose and wiped his spectacles he turned to Stephen.

'I got your note. It's all right. Hand it in sometime. Brr.' He turned to me. 'And how are you?'

I nodded as he had already turned back to Stephen.

'Had a good shoot?'

Stephen actually blushed with pride as he said, 'I bagged seven. Two are on the way to your house right now.'

'Ah, decent meal for once.'

He stared at the papers in his lap. As he did so the telephone rang. 'Yes, speaking,' he said. He listened. Glanced at me. Frowned. 'Yes, he is here. I've just begun my tutorial.' He listened again, staring gas-fire eyes at me. 'Yes, I'll tell him.'

'Were you supposed to see your Warden at nine o'clock?'

'First I've heard of it. You see, I did not check my mail. Survival instinct, I suppose.'

But the lame joke fell flat on its face. Its monkey face.

He blew brr brr. He said, 'You are to present yourself at his office as soon as this tutorial is over. It sounds very serious to me.'

'I honestly do not know what I am supposed to have done. I was drunk.'

Dr. Martins-Botha whistled through his teeth.

'I have heard about your drinking. Have you tried the AA?'

'I do not think they are the answer.'

'They could be a step towards it.'

'Perhaps.'

120

He opened his mouth to shout something but stopped and shook out his papers. I was thinking how All Souls' Day is also Walpurgisnacht. Just a fancy but it made me shiver. Stephen was smiling behind a cupped hand. He suddenly winked. When I did not wink back he exploded with laughter. The doctor, startled, looked up, stared hard at Stephen and grunted what to me sounded like a bad version of an ingratiating chuckle.

'Quite, ah quite. These things happen,' he said. Abruptly he turned to me. 'Begin.'

I picked up my essay from the floor and began to read. I was halfway through it when Dr. Martins-Botha laughed quite scornfully. I stopped. I did not look up. I waited until he had finished. I was about to resume when he suddenly—or was it Stephen's voice?—said, 'Nothing personal. You know.'

That is when I looked up. Dr Martins-Botha's right hand was between Stephen's thighs. They were both looking at me. I will always remember their eyes.

'Shall I go on?' I asked.

The doctor nodded. Once more I began to read. I know my face was quite impassive. But behind it I knew my brains had been touched by a thin slimy secret. It was as if an earwig was eating its way through my head. I finished reading. I felt very tired, very thirsty.

'That's it,' I said. And sank back into my chair.

'Well,' the doctor began. 'That's the best essay I've heard for years on the Gawain Poet. Have you any questions, Stephen?'

'It was brilliant. It quite settles everything,' Stephen said smiling. Christ. They were actually mocking me.

I gathered up my papers, stuffed them into my battered briefcase and stood up.

'Yes,' the doctor said, 'there is nothing else to be said. That's all for this week then. Ah, Stephen. I want your advice about something. Will you stay for a few minutes?'

'Of course.'

I do not know how I got there but I suddenly found myself standing in front of a triple whisky in the Monk's Bar at the Mitre. I drank two of those before I began to feel who I was waiting for in there. Margaret. She came in about ten minutes later. Her left hand was in plaster. Something that had always been intact in my mind suddenly tore at the sight of the plaster. Soon she saw me; she blew a kiss and was almost running as she made her way towards my table.

At last, something—not much—but something intensely personal was flying towards me like the flight of a burning sparrow.

The Sound of Snapping Wires

A mindless rage seized him. Boiling his brains. The police constable watched him warily. In the distance, behind the concrete wall, music boomed; hilarious shouts, voices enjoying themselves. He had been kicked out of the concert and had been trying to climb over the wall to gate-crash it through the back door. That is when the police constable made his knees tremble. He could smell the alcohol in his own breath. There was blood on his shirt-front, bloodstains from the fight in the concert. A cut above his left eye, a bruise on his right cheek-bone. He could still hear the feral grunts, the impact of the fists on his flesh and bone. One moment he was dancing; the next he was the centre of all the brute punches and kicks erupting from every direction. All those many black fists, those fiery blood-shot eyes homing down on him until finally they hurled him out, sending him sprawling on to his face and elbows. In the dark empty street he had picked himself up like a scruffy dog. And now here was the pig, in the guise of this young constable asking him his business.

The world was always asking him his business. The business in the concert had been about a girl. He did not even know her. He had just begun dancing with her on the packed floor. He had been dancing on his own all night and then suddenly she was beckoning to him swaying to his rhythm. He had not even thought about it. If you do without thinking the world will try to think out your business for you; with kicks and punches. And this policeman is trying to think out my climbing over this wall, and my blood-stained shirt-front.

It had been hell, the whole week. Alone in his flat eating semolina and soya beans. Trying to write his weekly poem. Feeling suffocated by the stale gas-fire air in the room. Trying to think out the pattern behind the deeds (or lack of them) in his own life. The flat was one of many in the miserable grey buildings off Clerkenwell Road; seedy graffiti, urine stains, shrieking cats. A gaunt derelict, dating back to the middle-nineteenth century, it housed a motley rabble of single persons, junkies, dope-pushers, frightened old-age pensioners, unemployed men and women. Most were either 'writers' or 'artists'. All suffered that inner city insecurity which had more to do with

122

a grimy mishandled fate than with financial problems. All week he had stayed in, reading endlessly, jotting down notes, refusing to open the front door if anyone knocked. He had started writing the kind of self-conscious 'ethnic' poetry which has its roots in a bogus vanity, employing the nuances of revolt and black pride. When he pared this down to the bone of his own personal experience, the anaemic imagery of self-analysis soón revolted him. Surely, he thought, a more than human event underlies all poetry, a more than human condition. But, of course, this too reeked of that degree of misanthropy which can paralyse the pen. By Friday night he was ready to give up. That is when he had gone to the African concert in Covent Garden. And now a policeman was roughly demanding an explanation which he himself had tried to wrestle into light all the days in his flat. And the pain in his chest probably meant that a rib or something had been fractured.

Go home and sleep it off,' the policeman had suggested. He tried to answer but only a horrible gurgling racked his throat. He spat a glob of blood. And staggered away. Friday night! What was there to go home to? True there were those books by Patricia Highsmith, P. D. James, and Dashiel Hammet. He had been reading only crime thrillers for months now. And those three authors were skilled enough to heal for hours on end the corrosive effects of loneliness. These days he no longer craved the company of other humans. It was too tiresome, too tedious. To enjoy another's company he had to drink himself into that illusory well-being which makes even the roughest contact a welcome and delirious thing. His watch said 1.30 a.m. He trudged up Charing Cross and stopped at the Kentucky Fried place. He joined the queue of black and white prostitutes who were slyly remarking his bloodied person. They understood and feared this violence which was an occupational hazard for them. Looking at them as the queue inched forward to the counter, he was aware of their sympathy for him, another victim creeping towards his package meal.

It was raining when he came out clutching his box of chips and spare ribs. The chill gusts blew hither and thither, billowing out his coat, hitting his face with the liquid globules of yet another indecisive London rain. He liked it.

This fresh and cold blast of sanity, soaking him already with its attendant sense of rootlessness, blew into his lungs and dragged out of him some of the night's bitterness. He drank every last drop of it. Before him was the tall YMCA building; immediately to his right was the illuminated fountain, the blue-green water sparkling upwards like a long-drawn-out yearning only to fall back to be recycled upwards once more. Like his own expectations. His own ambition—what had it been so long ago in high school and then at university? What was it? It had started in Africa and now found him here in London. Mooching his way in the small hours towards Clerkenwell Road. The wind and rain roared, splashed, spattered around him; it grew stronger reaching out its many arms to bowl him over. He leaned into it, walking like one wading against a strong undersea current. Listening to the heartbeat within, which was so like the sound of snapping wire. Guitar wires strummed too quickly, by the cynical chill of the small hours—they sang within and without him and he listened dreamily, eating the spare ribs and the chips in the city's dreary wetness. Behind him, and coming towards him, were other mysterious figures who could have been direct reflections of his own life.

Rain!

I am the rape

I am the rape
Marked on the map
The unpredictable savage
Set down on the page
The obsequious labourer
Who will never be emperor

My hips have rhythm
My lips an anthem
My arms a reckoning
My feet flight
My eyes black sunlight
My hair dreadlocks

Sit on this truth out at sea
Hit the shit when you go out to tea
Don't want to hear what ears hear
Don't want to see what eyes see
Your white body writhing underneath
All the centuries of my wayward fear

Goodness is not ground out of a stone
Evil neither. Men gnaw their chicken bones.
Know the electric shocks that seized my testicles.
Which now you eat with the lips of a sunrise
Your white body writhing underneath
All the centuries of my wayward fear.

Night on my Harmonica

The grime. The cheap and sordid details. That was my corner
of London. Off Gray's Inn Road. Its grit and dirt was ingrained
in my character. In my life. Four years of it. Yet I could think
of no other time, no other place, which attracted me as this one
did. Of course she believed in love. A cockroach may as well
swell and glow with absurd beliefs. In after life. In loyalty. In
paying one's debts. In keeping up with the rent. Those kind of
cheap and sordid details which are the channels through which
my life flows. Negatively. Christ, always negatively.

Most days I sit in my flat reading. I read everything. Dante,
James Hadley Chase, Shakespeare, Cervantes, de Sade, Al-
berto Moravia, Walter Pater, Playboy. I am usually broke. There
is no money for going out. She screams at me:

'You never take me anywhere. It's always the pubs. I'm sick
of the pubs!'

That was the other thing. Drink. I am always in the pub
buying the cheap joy pint by pint. Thanks to the Arts Council.
Which gives writers like me grants meagre enough to madden
us while working on the next novel. Bless them. But she thinks
I should not squander whatever talent I have got in writing
endless stories about anarchists and perverts and black writers
who have seen visions that condemn everything cheap and
sordid. And because I do not care what I do when I am drunk,
she accompanies me to the pubs. To see that I do not get into
trouble and end up in Brixton Prison, or get beaten up by people
I would have insulted, or squelch drunkenly under the wheels
of a double decker. We have had many arguments about this.
That I should stop drinking. I like drink. That okay I should
perhaps cut down on the pints. I do not want to. That I should
drink only wine. That is expensive and in any case wine does
not get me drunk in the way I like. That I should drink only at
home. I tried that twice and both times it frightened her.

I have told her to leave me many times. She will not listen.
And I have sometimes terrified her enough for her to grab her
things and run to stay with friends. Her friends have advised
her to leave me. She doesn't listen. Her mother has told her the
same thing. Her brother too. The times I wake up hungover and
find her not there I spend trying to remember if I hit her or if
I simply talked her into terror. I am very good at that. At talking

people into terror. The police have been a couple of times. She would be screaming and telling them to lock me up underground. But as always they simply shrug and say:

'It's a domestic matter.'

'But he's smashed up my guitar and my radio and my gram and tore up my dress!' she said.

They looked at me with distaste.

I was smoking another of yesterday's cigarette stubs.

'You can try the civil division but that's nothing to do with us.'

And they would leave. I would reach out for another bottle of Stingo. That time she began to cry, her head in her hands. I felt the hairs of my groin stirring. Was all this going on because of sex? Because she was white and I was piling up humiliations on her as revenge for all the years I spent under Ian Smith's boot? Was I a sadist? Or was I in some mad pursuit after the vain and complete possession? I remembered Albert Moravia's *The Empty Canvas*, a novel that tried to show 'the mania to possess, the impossibility of doing so, and the boredom which springs from this failure'. Did the same mechanism take place when the object to be possessed was a piece of land, a chunk of country to be grasped from the colonizer? Was I personally experiencing what in larger terms would overtake my newly independent country, Zimbabwe? In the form of corruption, power battles, administrative decay? A this point I pulled in the reins on my imagination. Had I not always said that everything was permitted that did not cause the other person pain? I threw the empty bottle into the far corner.

I was shaking.

Outside, the thunder of trucks, cars, loud heavy metal music. Screams as some prostitute was being beaten up. My neighbours were mostly squatters, dossers, derelicts, single parents who had given up. Young old men who passed themselves off as sculptors and painters. These now were my people. I was one of them. A down-and-out drifter who happened to write books. Something inside me tore. I shuddered. Two days ago it happened again. I was drunk and tried to end it all with the large kitchen knife. There was all this blood everywhere. I was more or less seeing the insides of my own ravings. I did not even see her go. I was trying to cut my own throat but I missed the vein. I am once more sitting in here, my neck thickly bandaged up, writing this very short story. Every time someone passes by the staircase I cock my head to listen. Thinking, hoping it is her come back. The electricity was cut off yesterday. I have these candles. I cannot watch the television. I am watching and waiting for her return.

Other published works by Dambudzo Marechera:

The House of Hunger. Zimbabwe Publishing House, Harare, latest edition 1990.

Black Sunlight. Heinemann, London, 1980.

Mindblast. The College Press, Harare, 1984.

Memorial publication:

Dambudzo Marechera 1952–87, edited by Flora Veit-Wild and Ernst Schade. Baobab Books, 1988.

✧

Works by other Zimbabwean writers published by Baobab and Academic Books in Harare:

Bones by Chenjerai Hove. Winner of the 1988–89 Zimbabwe Book Publishers' Association Literary Award and the Noma Award for Publishing in Africa, 1989. Baobab Books, 1988.

Harvest of Thorns by Shimmer Chinodya. 'A superb novel . . .' — *The Herald*. Baobab Books, 1989.

Stories from a Shona Childhood by Charles Mungoshi. Illustrated by Luke Toronga. Baobab Books, 1989.

Tales of the Secret Valley by Tim Matthews. Illustrated by Colleen Cousins. Baobab Books, 1988.

The Broken Promise – and other traditional fables from Zimbabwe, compiled by Norman Atkinson. Academic Books, 1990.

Vavariro by Raymond Choto. A novel in Shona. Baobab Books, 1990.

✧

See also:

Literature, Language & the Nation, studies in the role of literature and language in liberation and nation-building, edited by Emmanuel Ngara and Andrew Morrison. Baobab Books, 1989.

A People's Voice – Black South African Writing in the 20th Century by Piniel Shava. Baobab Books, 1990.